Never Say Too Late For Change

Never Say Too Late For Change:

Holding the team together

By
Dominic Ameri Itto, PhD.

Published by
Dominic A. Itto, PhD
204 Orchard Valley Drive
Smyrna, TN 37167
United States

This book is the work of fiction; any characters, places and organizations mentioned herein are fictitious imagination of the author, and do not represent real persons, organizations or places whatsoever. Any resemblance to actual places, organizations or persons living or dead is therefore coincidental.

Dedication

In memory of my late sister
Tiffania S. Itto.
You took me under your wings.
You made me who I am today.
I will always remember you.
I will always love you.
Your legacy will live forever.
You were my hero.

Prologue

Kim was unpleasant young female supervisor to work with from the very first day she came aboard. Her appointment as the new supervisor with child protection unit in the department of children services was a nightmare for Steve, Reggie and Tina. Kim was megalomaniac, bossy and uncompromising at workplace. Kim had fewer friends on the planet. Her arrogance and unfriendly behavior earned her more enemies at workplace and the neighborhood. Kim had maliciously attempted to use her fiancé's political position as leverage to intimidate the assistant commissioner of her department.

Her triangle love affair involving the fiancé, Congressman Devon Killinga, and his longtime friend Melvin Woodcock— commonly known as the Big Daddy was yet another defiance and betrayal after swindling Devon away from Katie—the closest friend she ever had.

However, despite Kim's relentlessness, and unfair treatment of her unit employees, the team neither gave up hope, nor quitted on her. They remained committed to helping Kim change into a better person. Kim miraculously responded, and made a dramatic change that took everyone by surprise. She opened up to accepting ideas and suggestions from her unit members. She reconciled with many individuals that deserted her earlier. Kim developed a sound managerial and leadership skills on the job and through training that served her well at the workplace in later days. Since her reinvention, Kim maintained fraternal relationship with Big Daddy, Steve, Katie and many others.

About The Author

I was born at Pageri, a small town in Southern Sudan. I had early education at Pageri, Loa and Juba, the capital city of South Sudan. I went to Rumbek Secondary school in 1973-1976. I joined Juba University/Sudan in 1978 where I graduated with a Bachelor Degree in Public Administration and Management in December 1982. I attended Graduate College/ University of Khartoum from 1994 to 1995 and obtained a Diploma in Development Studies.

Forced out of the country by the civil war in 1996, I fled to Syria where I lived as a refugee in the suburbs of Damascus for six months. I left Syria for Egypt to reunite with my family in January 1997, and lived there until June 1998. I seized the opportunity of the UNHCR resettlement program in 1997, and in 1998, I was resettled in the United States together with my family.

While in the United States; I worked two labor jobs to support the family. I also attended graduate school at Phoenix University, New Mexico where I graduated with MA Degree in Organizational Management in 2001. I earned my PhD. Degree in Public Policy and Administration from Walden University in May 2008. Currently I'm employed by the State of Tennessee in the Department of Human Services, Medicaid Policy Unit. My previous work history included South Sudan government, Norwegian Church Aid/Sudan program, Catholic Charities of Central New Mexico, and short term employment with private sectors.

Dominic Ameri Itto, PhD.

E-mail addresses: ditto@waldenu.edu
                       dominicitto@yahoo.com

Web site: www.ittobooks.com

Contents

Chapter One

The New Supervisor

The Child Protection Unit in the Department of Children Services was relatively calm and harmonious for Steve and four of his co-workers until a new supervisor took over the unit and turned it into hell on earth for some of its employees. It all started when the unit was detached from Child Adoption and Foster Care unit, and a supervisory position was created. A new supervisor was hired from within the department to head the unit. The director assumed the supervisor would bring in new talents and experience that would improve the quality of service delivery for the clients. Expectations and excitements were high. Every employee of the unit looked forward to cooperating with the new supervisor.

In the first week of the month, the program director called a unit meeting to introduce the new supervisor to her staff and their job assignments. The supervisor introduced herself as Ms. Kimberly, but said she only went by Kim. The staff introduced themselves in turns: Steve, Reggie, Tina, Amy, and Vicky. All were great workers and never had any troubles with the administration from before. But that had to change in the coming months as Kim consolidated power and instituted her new rules that made everyone in the unit nervous and unhappy.

Steve was hit the hardest. Perhaps Kim had singled him out for being a male. If that were the case, no doubt she could be allergic to men. That also raised the question of a boyfriend. Fortunately, she didn't have one. Otherwise, he could be the most unfortunate man ever to be crushed by this monstrous lady boss, whose attitude could discourage even the dumbest male on earth.

It wasn't immediately known what triggered her deviant behavior toward Steve and the other two female employees, Reggie and Tina. Kim worked hard to keep Vicky and Amy in her inner circle. She tried to use them as informants over activities of their co-workers, or "supervision by spying." The unit was already ailing as the divide-and-rule management style started to take its toll. The gap between the two groups got even wider and wider by the day. Kim never backed down with her megalomaniac supervision. She roamed from cubicle to cubicle to assert her new territory and areas for intimidations.

Steve, Reggie, and Tina remained devoted to their jobs. They took less and less interest to confront the supervisor. They soon learned the lack of supervisory competences and her unwillingness to learn new things from the subordinates triggered her aggressive attitude. To approach her for technical advice was like inviting harsh words and unprecedented assignments that were meant for her. She reported very early in the morning to record time of arrivals at the elevator area. She disputed everything from sick leave to annual leave requests. They even nicknamed her Ms. Luna (meaning lunatic).

Ladies couldn't withstand abuses from a female supervisor without getting dirty. Steve had already become immune. He paid less or no attention even when Kim yelled at the top of her voice, as she did all the time. Work hours became longer for Steve and two of his colleagues, but still they held their ground and performed their normal duties. Kim never gave up her mistreatment of the trio either. A day never passed without her coming after them for baseless and unfounded accusations.

The First Month

Kim called for a unit monthly meeting on Monday morning to distribute new assignments for her five employees. Steve walked Kim through all the kinds of work they did in the unit.

"I would like to reassign the jobs in this unit the way I think is best for everyone," said Kim.

She said this without communicating her staff of what she intended to do with their regular assignments.

"The director just distributed the assignments a month ago. Perhaps you have better to give it another two months or so to familiarize yourself with the kind of work we do here," said Steve.

The other staff members sat quietly gazing at the supervisor.

"I know what I'm doing. Why weren't you made the supervisor if you think you know better than I do?"

"Fewer chiefs than Indians," murmured Steve.

Kim scanned the department manual in front of her.

"I like that." Reggie lowered her head to avoid Kim.

"What did you just say, Steve?" Kim lifted her head and looked in his direction. "I know you have an issue with me." Kim angrily continued as if commanded to act defiantly.

"How could that possibly be? You have just joined this unit. We haven't yet gotten to know each other well." Steve brushed away her false accusation and wanted her to know he had no issues whatsoever.

Amy and Vicky kept aloof, but supportive of Kim.

A large volume of departmental policy manual still lay in front of Kim. She flipped the pages one after another to find an appropriate reference to quote, but, without any success, she then quickly got back to the forum furiously.

"Okay, y'all listen, and listen carefully. I don't give a damn with what you think. From today on, every one of you have to report directly to me."

She spelled out new guidelines and her standing orders. She distributed every bit of assignments, including her own to the subordinates. Steve realized the unfair job distribution that Kim had just assigned to them.

Then he quickly reacted. "Madame, the supervisor is supposed to handle all the referral cases from the county offices because you are the liaison between the state office and the various county offices. Are you trying to change the procedures now?" He waited for Kim to respond.

Kim looked at him with a taste of dislike. She frowned and tapped her pen on the table repeatedly to draw the attention of others in the room. She made sure everyone was listening. "Not only the procedures, but overhaul of the way you do things here altogether." She paused for a few seconds. "The procedures you referred to are not religious dogma and are therefore subject to change when deemed necessary." She stopped.

Her last statement disturbed Steve. He never expected Kim to be so rude and heartless in matters regarding team efforts.

"Madame, this is supposed to be a team-oriented work environment where each member has a part to play. Now, with this kind of work distribution, what role do you play as the contact person?"

Kim appeared more confrontational, but pretended as if his words never got into her nerves. She was, however, clear that time by using a harsh tone. "It's none of your business. I run the show." A little louder, she continued, "Have I made myself clear? You have gotten into my nerve this time, and I ain't gonna let that happen to me this time. Never ever." She was breathing fire beneath that nasty attitude. She wanted Steve to know who the boss was in the first place.

Amy and Vicky were whispering to one another.

Amy said in a low voice, "Gotcha."

"I like that. Let's see who is the boss," added Vicky.

Everyone in the room heard that. Steve, however, played it cool, but Reggie wouldn't buy that. She immediately sprang into action in his defense and attacked Vicky and Amy.

"Ass kissers, y'all fuck up." She stuck out one of her middle fingers as a warning sign.

Amy and Vicky zipped up their mouths at once. Amy and Vicky knew Reggie very well. It wouldn't take long to get her really furious. She once banged Amy's head against the bathroom sink. They knew they had to be careful, or she would do it again if things got out of hand.

Kim intervened. Reggie eventually calmed down.

Kim took the stage once again. "I'm here to manage and put in place the mess you created while the lead person misled your co-workers and created a state of confusion. And nothing else. Do y'all understand and know the mess he created in this unit?" Kim said to her divided staff.

Amy and Vicky snarled over their shoulders and laughed quietly in praise of Kim.

"That's not a leadership position for God's sake. You're a hands-on supervisor who had to give us the support we may need on technical matters." Steve knew what Kim intended to impose on them: fear, control, subjugation, and intimidation.

It took the group an hour to wind up their meeting. Steve, Reggie, and Tina left the conference room immediately after the meeting was over. Kim, Amy, and Vicky remained behind in the conference room.

Tina stayed right by the door of the conference room. She overheard Vicky say, "That was insubordination, you know. He had no right to question you on the kinds of assignments you should do."

"He thinks he's a man. Maybe I'll back down whenever he threatened me. I'm from the Deep South, and y'all know that we don't blink in the face of enemies. I won't give a damn. I'll make this unit a hell on earth should I choose to. I'll make his life very miserable, like beggars on the streets of Calcutta."

Both Vicky and Amy laughed earnestly amidst phrases in support of her.

"You're my girl," said Vicky.

Amy quickly added, "You go, girl."

The three laughed aloud. Kim looked at her watch. It was twenty minutes past their scheduled time, "Girls, could we leave the room for the next group?" Kim asked, and the two ladies consented, then they walked out of the conference room one after another with Kim first and Amy and Vicky following closely after. Once outside the conference room, they noticed Tina was still by the door. One of her friends had joined her. Amy giggled as they walked past Tina.

"What was that supposed to mean?" Tina's friend turned around to take a good look at Amy, Vicky, and Kim.

"Our new supervisor and her confidants." Tina made a hand sign to let her friend ignore them.

"What's your supervisor's name? She doesn't look familiar to me."

"Call her Kim."

"Kimberly. Is that right?"

"Yep, but she only goes by Kim. Very interesting, isn't it?"

"What difference does it make?" The difference in Kim's name made no sense to her.

"It sounds exotic for her, like the Korean name."

The friend laughed. Tina excused herself and rushed to the office before Kim could make her next round of the roll call. Reggie and Steve were already prepared to take their first break when Tina got there. The three decided to leave together for the break.

"I have just declared that in the meeting a while ago. I'll only allow short breaks on an individual basis and not for a group to take break at the same time. Take my warning seriously, and let me know if you have any concerns." Kim tried to stop the three from leaving for their fifteen-minute break together.

"We're just fine, girls. Let's just get out of here. We will know how to answer her by the time we come back," Steve said.

They walked away from their cubicles. Kim rushed to the director's office as she usually did, but, unfortunately, the director wasn't in the office. She went to Vicky's cubicle, but she wasn't there either. She was out for her fifteen-minute break with Amy. Their absence made it very uncomfortable for Kim to pursue a case against Steve, Reggie, and Tina for undermining her orders. She hurriedly went back to her office and sent an e-mail with a copy to the director. "I'm utterly disappointed with your unruly behaviors and lack of discipline in this unit. I have said it before, and I will reiterate that employees shouldn't leave their cubicles without my approval. Take my words seriously."

Kim concluded her message with strong wordings that read, "I'll not tolerate any defiant behavior in this unit, and y'all have to adhere to this standing order."

The director returned to her office after the meeting and got Kim's disturbing e-mail.

She immediately wrote back to Kim, "What was all that for? Can't you just use a mild language to address this issue?" The director had warned Kim of using harsh language when sending out e-mail from before.

Steve and the two girls came back after ten minutes. Kim had already positioned herself to monitor the time of their return from the break. She was disappointed to see them come back five minutes ahead of their allowed fifteen minutes.

While in the office, the director referred another case to Kim for immediate action. Kim quickly assigned Steve to research the case and get the result back to her. Steve did the research and sent the findings to her and a copy to the director. That disappointed Kim.

She went to Steve. "Who told you to send a copy to the director without my authorization? I asked you to research, not to distribute copies."

She cursed and yelled at the top of her voice for everybody to hear as she stood outside Steve's cubicle. Even employees in other units knew her provocative attitude.

Steve was quiet. Kim felt like he had ignored her, so she decided to leave. She went around and ended up in the cubicle of her friend in another unit.

"Hello! The boss lady," the friend said as Kim popped into the cubicle without prior notice.

"I'm not in good mood today." Kim stood still with hands akimbo.

"You look kinky. What's the matter?" She asked Kim just to make sure she wasn't in serious trouble.

"That son of a bitch drove me crazy." Kim waited and expected the friend to offer her a seat, but, unfortunately, she never did, so Kim reluctantly placed herself on a chair that barely supported her weight.

"Why would you let that happen to you, sweetie pie." Her friend pretended to be nice and sympathetic.

"I'm just bidin' my time. I gonna show him my true color when I kick his ass," said Kim with sort of exaggerated strength.

"Give him a hard time instead. No, that's still not enough. Give him a real heart attack this time. Keep him on his toes. Summon him in your office every thirty minutes. That way, he'll get to know who's in charge."

"I don't wanna see his face in my office that many times." Kim dismissed the suggestion.

"Then stare at his behind if that would make you any happier." She laughed again and again for the remarks.

"I better not call him in my office at all and that's it."

"It's cute, isn't it?" said the friend provocatively. She was picking on Kim rather than offering moral support.

"You better answer that yourself."

Disappointed, Kim left her friend's cubicle. The friend didn't offer her the support she needed most. Kim retreated and went back to her cubicle, still feeling tense and deranged. She opened up her e-mail and found that another urgent case was referred to her from the field office. It had to be researched and resolved immediately. She quickly forwarded that one to Steve as well. "Here is another case I want to see researched, make it a first priority. Send your findings to me, and let me warn you, no copy to the director this time." She wrote in her e-mail

Steve was already overwhelmed with pending caseloads marked as urgent. "Ma'am, I have over ten cases on priority list, I would better research them in the order of receipt." He replied to Kim's e-mail.

Kim yelled like a cheater caught with another man. She came to Steve and stood outside his cubicle. "I wanna see this case researched now and the findings to be on my desk within the next hour." She paused and took a deep breath. "Have I made myself clear?"

Kim ordered Steve to research the case over his lunchtime. Steve chose not to argue with her. Then she left for her cubicle, but immediately came back when she saw Reggie and Tina walking toward Steve's cubicle. The three had already left when she got there. Disappointed, she went back to her office.

"My world is falling apart, Kim keeps pilling new cases on the already mounted caseloads that need to be researched today." Steve told Reggie and Tina.

"That's unfortunate, but we are available should you need our help," said Reggie.

"Remember, we are a team," added Tina, as she moved closer to Steve and gently patted him on the back.

Kim, however, acted very swiftly, well before the three got back from lunch. Steve received an e-mail from Kim and she wrote, "You failed to submit your findings as instructed by your superior. I need a full explanation within an hour as to why you ignored my request." the message was brief and intimidating.

Steve wasted no time, in his response he wrote; "I was on my lunch break, besides, there was no way I could have research the case. He also copied the director in his reply to Kim.

Kim was disappointed. She rushed to Steve's office and confronted him. "What do you think you are? Why do you keep undermining her authority as the supervisor by copying the director in your e-mail?" But Steve repeatedly ignored her. Kim felt stupid, then she left.

The director called for a meeting the next day to resolve the dispute.

In the meeting, Kim accused Steve of insubordination and poor performance. Steve defended himself. He complained of the supervisor's arrogance, poor judgment, and draconian supervisory style. The meeting ended without any compromise or amicable solution.

Two days later, Steve requested three days of annual leave to escape Kim's unprecedented attitude against him. Immediately after receiving Steve's request, Kim rushed to his cubicle and then confronted him.

"You have accumulated a helluva compensatory leave hours. You better exhaust that first before you request time off against your annual leave." Kim uttered and then paused. "Make another leave request against the compensatory leave balance. I'll review it to see if it would be okay for me to grant you one or two days."

She left his cubicle and swerved her butt left and right as she walked. A newly hired secretary watched speechlessly as Kim walked past the wide-open cubicle. Kim waited impatiently for another e-mail from Steve, but he never sent one. Kim was even more agitated. She decided to go back to Steve.

She started to yell at him from afar. "Where's the e-mail I asked you to send me? Do it now or else I'll change my mind and recommend whoever applies for leave before you."

"I already made my request in writing, and you haven't responded to it yet." Steve actually didn't want verbal confrontations.

He wanted Kim to commit herself in writing, and she, in stupidity, did that.

"Steve, your behavior is intolerable and despicable," she wrote. "I tried to make your request excusable and be charged against your compensatory leave hours. How dare you expect me to coach you to make a simple request by e-mail?" She ended her message by stating, "You better comply, or you rot, you fucker!"

Steve got his wish. He printed the e-mail and went with it straight to the director. She also acknowledged that it was inappropriate and unprofessional. She summoned Kim to her office and explained some procedures and policies that she needed to follow when communicating to her employees. The director made it clear that derogatory language and use of uppercase and bolded letters in e-mail was offensive and shouldn't be used for communicating with the subordinates or clients at every level.

The first month showed Kim's true colors. A day never passed without confrontation with Steve. Weekdays were like long and exhaustive court days for Steve. He became deranged, and he repeatedly forfeited even his break times to complete some of his mounting assignments. Kim kept pounding him with additional cases. Steve was devastated and stressed out. He had been to counseling with Employee Assistance Program (EAP) twice already, and he thought the third counseling wouldn't do him any better either.

Kim stepped up her campaign. She kept telling her friends and associates how she stubbornly managed to keep Steve under control and brought him down to his knees.

"He thought he was tough and tried to defy my orders. That won't happen if I'm still around as the supervisor of the unit. He's now seeking counseling for mental evaluation, poor little thing." Kim said loudly in order for Reggie and Tina to hear.

"How did you do that, girl?" asked her associate.

"I gave him stern orders to observe. I'll kick his ass if he doesn't comply."

"Why can't you and Steven or whoever try to resolve your differences peacefully?" one associate suggested. "Have you ever tried that?"

"Don't even suggest that. Steve should know why I'm in that unit and what he's to begin with. A guy like Steve needs no leniency. He thinks he's playing tough and not knowin' that I can bring him down whenever I choose to."

The associate knew that Kim was short-tempered and pompous. She was a slow learner and uncompromising when things got physical. She wondered how Kim was offered that sensitive position from among all the competent and professional candidates who would have managed the unit quite successfully. Kim had never supervised before. She had never been exposed to working with a talented team in a challenging work environment. What she needed most was to surround herself with people with talents to acquire the necessary skills that would offer her the opportunity for effective supervision.

Chapter Two

The Second Month

Kim had consolidated her power and authority over the unit. She looked forward to celebrating her success of bringing Steve under her feet. Nothing was better for her than to see Steve confined in his miserable cubicle with his eyes glued to the computer screen, endlessly researching the most difficult cases he had ever encountered in his career with the unit. Steve saw no daylight until he got off work to catch the bus, which then took him an hour and half or more to get home. He woke early in the morning Monday through Friday to catch the bus that brought him to the workplace. The bus drivers knew him by name. They wouldn't leave their bay for ten extra minutes if they knew Steve wasn't on the bus yet for his regular ride home.

The monthly conference came too soon for Steve, who didn't need a distraction from the assignments and their deadlines. Kim had sent a memo for the unit staff to inform them of the date and time for the conference. She stressed that all should attend the two-hour conference. All had accepted, and Kim marked that down in her favorite calendar book she called the "black book." Kim never left the book on the desk. It was either in her hand or inside the oversized handbag that contained everything from makeup to junk snacks.

Kim was the first to arrive in the conference room, she expected other members to be there ahead of schedule. She waited for a good fifteen minutes before the other members showed up, and Steve was the last to arrive. Kim was breathless, but took no action.

Kim cleared her voice and then gave her opening speech. "Y'all know this is our second conference in this month. From now on, I'll schedule our conferences at the end of every month to discuss your progress in this unit. I'm so excited and proud of myself for the progress and changes I have made in this unit."

Then she continued to talk about additional procedures she planned to introduce. She literally went through the whole agenda before she settled down to her core third topic.

"Y'all go to topic number three of this agenda and read aloud some of the rules I want everyone to follow and respect."

"Steve!" she called. Steve lifted his head to hear what she had to say. "Could you read rule number one for the rest of your colleagues?"

Steve straightened himself and read the first line of the third topic. "Effective immediately, employees should never use the office phone for private calls." He stopped.

Reggie, could you read for us the second line? Kim asked

Reggie sprang up and read, "No loitering during working hours. Visits should be limited to official business only. Remember, no excuses whatsoever." Reggie sat down.

Kim moved ahead and looked in Tina's direction. "Next one, read the third line for us." She pointed at Tina, who was ready to start reading.

Tina read loudly, "An employee should never leave his or her cubicle without permission from the departmental supervisor." She came to a stop.

Kim responded right away. "Wow! That was so loud, but thanks anyway." The group laughed. "Hush! You are next, Vicky. Let's hear if you will be as loud as that one." Kim's remark insulted Tina.

"Employees should never eat lunch or snacks at their workstations." Vicky stopped. Before she sat down, she asked Kim, "Was I being loud like her?"

"No, cutie pie, that was wonderful. Please sit down, and let's hear from Amy." She paused, then said; " Amy, please stand up and read the fifth line."

Amy was a bit nervous, as she always was, but she got up. With the agenda sheet in both hands, she read, "Government computers are for office use only and so is the Internet. The supervisor has the jurisdiction to check the computer portals of every employee in this unit to make sure employees are in compliance with the rule."

Amy looked terrified for the first time. She felt like the honeymoon was ending. She shrugged and then hurriedly took her seat. There were still three rules that had yet to be read, and Kim asked; "Any volunteers to read the remaining three lines or so? The room was quiet, it seemed no one was interested in doing so.

"Steve or Stephen, whatever you prefer to be called," she said carelessly. "Read the sixth line for us."

Steve looked left and right to make sure he didn't raise his hand. "But I didn't raise my hand, did I?" he responded jokingly.

But, unfortunately, Kim missed the message, and she immediately sprang on him. "I said, read line number six for us. This is an order from your supervisor."

"Okay, boss lady! I'm at your service." Steve then started to read the sentence. "Observe the core work hours. An employee should not log on to his or her computer before seven o'clock if he or she works from seven o'clock to three thirty. Log off the computer at exactly three thirty, and leave the office immediately." He stopped and sat down.

"Don't ever refer to me like that. I'm not your mama's boss. I'm your supervisor, and you have to look at me as such. Have I made myself clear?" She still stared at Steve in an unusual way, as she always did.

"Sounded like you have made your point, boss," said Steve.

"Now, who wants to read the next rule?"

No one responded, and Kim pointed in Reggie's direction. "Read line seven and I'll read the last one." She still looked at Reggie as she prepared to read the seventh rule. "You can remain seated if you prefer to." Kim commented.

Reggie did just that as she read the seventh line. "Strictly observe the state employees dress code. No to baggy pants, cowboy hats, mini shirts, and sneakers. All indecent clothes and bras are not allowed as well."

Kim sprang up immediately after Reggie was done to demonstrate what the ladies should wear. "This is what I mean by professional outfit." She spread her hands wide open to let the employees see her pants and waistcoat. "Take my example to aspire the way you dress and look."

"Ugh! We can't do it exactly the way you look. We prefer some kinda privacy," Tina said, referring to Kim's wide-open zipper that revealed her tiny underwear.

Amy moved swiftly from her seat and whispered into Kim's ear, "You need to zip up your pants, ma'am."

Kim looked down to her. Then she immediately took off and ran toward the ladies' restroom to fasten the zipper. It never worked. The pin ripped off, and she couldn't find it. Vicky followed her into the bathroom and found Kim distressed. She didn't know what to do. Vicky left Kim there and went to her cubicle. She immediately went back with a safety pin for Kim to clip the zipper together. Then they went back to join the group in the conference room.

"I'm so sorry that happened to me at the very wrong time. Gosh! I wish I checked it before exposing myself to you. I'm so embarrassed."

Everyone was quiet. That sent Kim a bad message. She looked in Steve's direction.

"I took little notice though, but you look great, ma'am. You sincerely do." He went quiet again.

Kim smiled. At last the man she hated had complimented her even for the mess she made.

"Thanks, Steve, for the compliments. Believe me, that will be the first and the last. You will never ever see me exposed like that again." She laughed. Soon, the rest in the room joined her.

"You never know. Another good day might come around again," Steve commented. Reggie pointed a finger at him. "Oops! Did I say something?"

He guessed Reggie was warning him not to develop some kind of interest in Kim. Before Reggie could respond, however, Kim jumped in headlong, "You're fine. Let's proceed with the meeting. Oh Lord! That was not funny." Kim recalled her gaffe, but never slowed down.

"All right, folks. Let me read the last but not least rule for you." She remained seated and read the last line on the agenda. "Be orderly and respectful to your co-workers. Be guided by the training you had in respectful workplace." She was very brief and never completed reading the whole content of rule number eight. She instead gave comment after comment on the use of appropriate language, sexism, inappropriate remarks, and many more. Time had run out, and she abruptly closed the meeting.

"I'm sorry. We can't continue with our meeting as you can see. You can, however, e-mail any of your questions … constructive questions … to me, and I'll get back to you as soon as possible. Remember, however, I will respond to any question in the order of receipt." She let everyone leave the room except Vicky, whom she asked to remain behind.

"Am I in trouble, supervisor?" Vicky moved closer to Kim.

"Did I say that, Vicky?" Kim reached out and touched Vicky's shoulder. Vicky placed her left hand over Kim's, and both smiled.

"No, I'm just curious," Vicky was relieved to learn she wasn't in trouble.

"I just wanted to thank you for getting my pants fastened. I was kinda embarrassed for the mess I made."

"It wasn't as bad as you might think. The underwear was so cute, and I saw Steve secretly staring in that direction."

"Really! I couldn't imagine that myself."

"Aw yeah! I kinda like it."

"Thank you so much, Vicky. But what interested Steve to look at things underneath my pants?"

Vicky shrugged. "Don't ask me. You better ask him." She paused. "Maybe he liked it." She burst into laughter.

"What are you laughing at, Vicky?"

Vicky came to a sudden halt. "That tiny thing is really cute, isn't it?"

Kim was thrilled. She wanted to hear more praises of that kind. She asked Vicky again and again of whether that impressed Steve. Vicky assured her a couple times that any man wouldn't take his eyes off her without pleading for a second chance. Kim felt satisfied. They vacated the room for another group that was already impatiently waiting outside. Kim apologized to the group for keeping them waiting for so long.

Reggie and Tina got together and digested the rules delivered upon them. Then both left with anger and disappointment.

"The break room is always full. Where does she want us to have our lunch?" Tina couldn't figure out what to do.

"Those damn rules were just bogus. I don't take them seriously."

"I'll eat my lunch inside the cubicle, as other employees of the department do. I'd like to see what she's gonna do." Tina was determined to confront Kim on that particular rule. She was certain that even the directors ate inside their cubicles to save time.

"You go, girl! Let's just do that. I got you covered."

They got their lunches from the refrigerator, warmed them up, and then went to Tina's cubicle, where they had lunch. Steve was nowhere to be seen, but Reggie and Tina found out that he and Kim were in training together. The training was scheduled to end at three thirty, but the tutor was ahead of schedule. She let the trainees leave at three fifteen. Steve and many others left for home. Kim went back to the office and noticed Steve was not there at three thirty.

She immediately sent an e-mail to him, "Steve, you left for home before your scheduled work hours this evening without permission from your supervisor. This is absolutely unacceptable. You must explain in writing why you did that." She signed her name and sent the e-mail at three fifty.

Steve came to work the next morning, only to find that Kim was already in the office since six twenty to monitor time of arrivals for Steve, Reggie, and Tina. Steve arrived at six fifty. Reggie and Tina arrived shortly after.

"Let everybody put down seven o'clock on your timesheet. Don't log on to your computers until seven o'clock. Steve, I have sent you an e-mail, and you never replied it." She made another gaffe again. She forgot that her e-mail went out after the official work hour.

"It's not yet seven. Besides, I can't read your e-mail if I'm not logged in."

"Reply to my e-mail as soon as you log in to your computer this morning." She checked the logbook to see if the three had put down the right time (seven o'clock) before she walked away toward her cubicle.

Steve waited until seven o'clock to log on his computer. He checked the mail and got Kim's message. He printed the message and walked straight to her cubicle then he asked; "Can we talk about this message please? He put the message on the desk in front of Kim.

She looked up at Steve and arrogantly said; "Get lost; I don't have time to discuss any of your concerns.

"Schedule an appointment if you have anything to discuss with me. This isn't an animal zoo where visitors loiter at leisure." She grumbled.

Steve was deeply hurt. He couldn't expect such words could come from someone who was supposed to be his supervisor. Steve withdrew without uttering a word. He went back to his cubicle.

Fifteen minutes later, Kim showed up in his cubicle. "Why are you undermining my authority? I want a reply to my e-mail in writing now." She stood outside his cubicle and threw word after word at him.

"How do you expect him to reply to you when you stand over him yelling?" Reggie didn't appreciate Kim's approach of dealing with subordinates.

"What did you just say, you little rat?" Kim turned her anger toward Reggie. She paused for a few seconds. "Look at you. You better go and take a good look of yourself in the bathroom mirror." Kim wasn't only an arrogant supervisor. She was like a human storage for nasty words. Her words could set a house on fire.

"Aw yeah! You better think twice. We know you have paid a heavy price to get that position. Cheap, trigging girl."

Reggie was quick-tempered and prepared for a fistfight, but Tina calmed her down and led her away from the scene and back to her cubicle. Kim took to her heels when she heard the director talking to another employee close by. Reggie was also quiet and so were Steve and Tina. The director walked past the cubicles of the three. She seemed busy and unconcerned with the things outside her schedule.

Still restless, Kim sat in her office. She wanted to confront Reggie, but couldn't do so. She hurriedly left her office and asked Vicky to accompany her to Walgreen's. They left, and Kim had nothing other than to tell Vicky what had happened between her and Reggie that morning.

"For real! Did she want to fight you because you talked to Steve?" Vicky asked.

"Why should I lie to you? She swung on me just like that." Kim clipped her left fingers to demonstrate how Reggie jumped on her.

"I told you. She's having an affair with Steve. Do you believe me now?" She patted Kim on the back as they walked.

"It looks like it, but let's not jump to any conclusion at this time." Kim lowered her strides to keep pace with Vicky.

"Whatever. You'll learn it more by yourself one day." Vicky was somewhat disappointed.

"Can you do me a favor? I want you to keep an eye on them. Listen to what they say about me, and report it to me."

"What! You mean like spy on them for you?" That malicious assignment was ridiculous. Vicky reacted sharply. She felt uncomfortable with the sort of thoughts Kim wanted to draw her into.

"You can call it so." Kim didn't clarify why she wanted Vicky to carry out that risky mission.

"I don't think I'm the right person for that job." Vicky didn't like to get into that kind of business. She knew very well that leaders come and go, and Kim would not be the exception.

"Fine. I can't force you against your will." Kim backed away from convincing Vicky to take the assignment.

"Thank you for understanding. I can do anything for you except this one. I'm not comfortable with it."

"Promise me that you'll never tell this to anyone." Kim was frightened.

"I promise. You also promise me that you won't assign me this kind of mission again in the future."

"Deal! I promise never to get you involved with matters of this nature. Are you happy now?" Kim assured her.

"Not really. I've turned down my boss." But Vicky was grateful to strike a deal with Kim over that mission.

"Maybe you'll change your mind and still carry it out for me, your friend." Kim gently rubbed Vicky's back.

"I guess not, not with this particular case." Vicky rejected categorically. She knew it was a dangerous game, and she could lose her job when discovered.

They abandoned the topic as they approached the drugstore. Kim got some cleaning stuff and some snacks, her favorite bag of spicy pork skins and energy bars. They went back to the office with essentially no discussion until they got into the building. Kim tried to offer some snacks to Vicky as they were about to separate.

"No, thanks. I am on Weight Watchers," said Vicky.

"Aw yeah! I didn't know that. Okay, now only take one of the drinks if you don't mind." She handed one can of Diet Coke to Vicky.

"Thanks. This is enough for me." Vicky started to walk toward her cubicle.

"No problem. See ya later!"

Vicky disappeared from where they were. "Oh, man! What was she doing?" Vicky muttered to herself.

She had never done such a dumb thing before, not even for money, let alone the free service just to satisfy her supervisor's ill intention. She thought deeper and deeper for a while, but never reached a concrete conclusion. She immediately brushed away the idea from her mind to concentrate on her own business. She never drank the Coke. She felt like it was a bribe to keep her mouth shut. Vicky never spoke to Kim that whole week, but Kim never let her slip away that easily.

One morning, Kim asked Vicky to join her for lunch with a friend, but, fortunately, Vicky had a doctor's appointment that day and had to leave early.

"I have a doctor's appointment at twelve thirty. Don't you remember?"

"I remembered I did approve your sick leave request, but I forgot the date." Kim was still doubtful of the date.

"Yep, it's today. I'm sorry about that, Kim." Vicky pretended as if she would have loved to join her for the lunch when she really hated even seeing Kim in her cubicle.

"I'm sorry, too. I wish we could make it together. Maybe next time," Kim lamented, looking disappointed.

"Let's hope so." Vicky got up from the chair to show some respect to Kim, who already conceded any further attempts.

Kim left Vicky's cubicle and went back to her office, trying to figure out whom to go with. She had told her friend earlier that she was coming with one of her co-workers. She couldn't convince Amy to join her for the lunch without Vicky, so she called her friend to inform her about a change in plan.

"Hello, Katie. It's me, Kim." She waited for her response.

After few seconds or so, Katie answered, "Hi, Kim. I'm sorry. I was away from my phone. What's goin' on?"

"Nothin' much. Just wantin' to let you know we may not be able to meet over lunch today. Can you fix another day, please?"

"Absolutely. How about tomorrow?"

"That's too soon. Make it for next week or so." Kim wanted to make sure she had tapped either Vicky or Amy to be in her company.

"That's fine with me. Give me some time to come up with the date."

Kim felt a bit easier.

"Can you hold on a few seconds? I've got someone calling."

"Sure! Call me when you are ready," Kim gladly responded. She immediately said to herself, "Yes, I'll make sure I get one of them to join me when the time comes." She placed the phone back on the base and went back to the computer. The phone rang. She picked it up. It was Katie once again.

"I am sorry about that. A co-worker called. I for sure will call you once the date is fixed, and you have a great day."

"You do the same. Bye-bye." Kim hung up.

Vicky left early that day for her doctor's appointment. Amy left for lunch with one of her friends from another unit just in time before Kim could catch up with her. Kim had ill advised her one time to do what it took in order to secure promotion in the unit, and she considered that inappropriate.

"I tell you, Amy. Promotion don't come easy nowadays. You should exercise your mind and body in order to get what you want."

"That isn't ethical. Besides, promotions are supposed to be by merit."

"Aw yeah! Who told you that?" Kim questioned. She continued before Amy could say even a word. "Listen to me, baby girl. Ethical or not, you need promotion, period." Kim tried to persuade Amy to accept her ill-intended advice, but Amy backed off.

"I've been on this job for over three years. Besides, I'm not in a hurry for any sort of promotion yet."

"Sorry. I didn't know that, but it makes no difference to me. I was in this department for four years when I got my first promotion and now this supervisory position as well." Kim smiled, which neither moved nor swayed Amy.

"Some people are born lucky. They get what they want without laboring for it."

Amy's response didn't resonate well with Kim. She quickly fired back, "Low-life people don't think out of the box. That's exactly what they always say."

She excused herself after making that remarks and left, leaving Amy to deal with whatever pain the last statement would have caused her.

Since then, Amy tried to keep her distance from Kim. She never told Vicky about that encounter, and she seemed not ready to disclose it to her either.

Chapter Three

The Third Month

Three months had passed since Kim had assumed the office of unit supervisor. She continued to abuse her powers and never reckoned to involve her subordinates in decision-making processes. She instead wrote up Steve without any verbal warning. Her excessive control made every employee unhappy and worried of his or her future with the workplace once considered to be a second home. She falsely accused Steve of keeping porn magazines in his drawer, although what she actually saw was a male bodybuilding magazine. Steve reported the case to the director with a copy to Kim. The director called a meeting to resolve the dispute. Kim was asked to produce the magazine. She gladly went and got the magazine from Steve's drawer and then handed it over to the director.

"Is this the very magazine you saw on his desk?" asked the director.

Kim opened her eyes wide open in excitement. "Positive! That's what I saw him looking through."

She stopped. On the front page of the magazine, however, was a picture of a man with massive body muscles wearing a typical sports suit, and it wasn't offensive by any count.

"Do you agree that what Kim saw in your office was this magazine?" The director asked Steve, who was shaking his head because of Kim's senseless allegation.

"That's correct, ma'am. I borrowed it from fitness center where I exercise. You can look at the slip inside the magazine," said Steve.

The director flipped over a couple pages and found the slip. The return due date for the magazine was the next day. The director then met with Kim and Steve separately and declared the magazine wasn't porn. Finally, Steve felt at ease and put his bitterness behind him. Vicky and Amy were upset when they learned of the allegation about Steve, but said nothing.

"I knew he took off some pages of the naked women." Kim told Katie on the phone one day.

"Sports magazines don't carry porn pictures. You can find ladies in fancy mini bikinis, but it doesn't necessarily mean exposure for pornography." Katie talked to her at length and tried to advise Kim on how to show leadership and good judgment over sensitive matters.

"Okay, Katie, I heard you."

She wanted to cut their conversation short, but Katie wouldn't let her go. "Have you apologized to Steve about your misjudgment? You better do so if you haven't yet."

"Why should I?" Kim was agitated. Besides, she was not the kind of person who could distinguish between right and wrong.

"You wrote him up for a wrong cause, didn't you?" Katie tried to make sure Kim understood what she did was wrong.

But Kim didn't give a damn. "I was right, and my action was in place. He never responded to the explanation letter. How do you explain that?" Kim asked in a rather coarse voice.

"Consider the explanation letter as null and void. Don't even refer to it, my dear friend."

"I know the director sided with him. That wasn't the first time she preferred Steve's suggestions over mine. I suspect something is wrong somewhere."

"Exactly! Something is wrong with your poor judgment, and you need to work on that. The earlier, the better. Let me take you for lunch at the Italian restaurant on Mission Avenue this coming Friday. Will that be okay with you?"

"Friday won't be a good day for me. We have leadership training for the whole day." Kim didn't have training that Friday, but she was simply upset with Katie for her criticisms. Kim even planned to boycott seeing her altogether.

"I'm so happy for you. That training will help you a lot to become a better supervisor. We'll schedule another day if you still want us to hang out together." Katie's time was running out, so she let Kim go.

A week later, Katie bumped into Kim in a Mexican restaurant during lunchtime. Kim was seated by the window and eating chicken enchilada when Katie sat down at the same table and faced Kim.

"Hello, sunshine. How are you doing?" asked Katie.

Kim smiled. "Hi, dear. Long time no see."

"I was kinda busy compiling some financial reports for the external audits." Katie used both hands to draw her chair closer to the table.

"I see. That must be a tedious and time-consuming assignment." Kim never expected to meet with Katie that soon.

"Yeah, it was, but, thank God, I'm done with it for now." Katie looked at Kim for a moment. "How was your training? I hope it went well." She had no idea of how tough Kim was in creating stories.

"It was wonderful. I kinda liked it. I look forward to attending the second phase of the training." Kim lied.

Katie immediately knew something was wrong with Kim's statement. She had learned earlier from one of their friends that Kim was with her at the mall that Friday. But she wanted to catch Kim in her own lies. She decided to ask Kim something that would get her off balance. "Who was with you in the training? I remember Peter and Denise were other participants from my department."

"Yeah! We had four from our department, and Steve was one of them. Denise left a little earlier that day," she happily stated.

Katie laughed. She had caught her friend red-handed, and she concluded that Kim was deceptive and a liar. She, however, never disclosed it to Kim right out. They ate and talked until it was time for them to leave. Katie volunteered to pay the bill for both, but Kim rejected the offer.

"No, you can't do that." Kim had wanted to square it herself, but Katie never let that happen.

"Yes, I can. Remember I asked to take you for lunch last week if not for your training? Now I have got to square this right here." Katie grabbed both bills, walked down to the cashier, and paid them off.

They came out of the restaurant, walked together for a short distance, and then separated to go to their office buildings.

Kim got to the office and immediately realized she had made a terrible mistake for lying to Katie. She was with one of Katie's friends at the mall that Friday afternoon, and she would have probably told Katie about it. She tried to reach Katie twice by phone, but Katie didn't pick up. That made Kim even more nervous. She tried to reach her on the office phone, but dialed the wrong number.

"Hello, how can I help you?" the lady answered.

"Yes, ma'am. I am trying to reach Katie. Can I talk to her, please?" Kim was desperate and wanted to get in touch with Katie by all means.

"Whom am I speaking with?" The lady's voice was getting tense and confrontational.

"My name is Kim."

The word "Kim" got into the ears of the lady like she was splashed on the face with boiling oil. She screamed at the top of her voice, and Kim wasn't even able to hang up the phone.

"Are you the same Kim calling my husband again? Not this time, girl. I gonna kick your ass, you bitch!" She screamed and hurled insults that Kim herself was not able to remember.

"I'm so sorry. I got the wrong person." She hung up. "Shit, shit, shit!" Kim said to herself. She was hysterical. She kicked repeatedly against her cubicle wall so hard that another employee in the next cubicle ran to find out what was happening.

"Are you all right, ma'am?"

Kim drew in a heavy breath. "Yes, I'm fine. Thanks for asking."

Kim didn't look too happy. "Can you leave me alone for a little bit?"

The lady left at Kim's request and went back to her cubicle. Kim remained low-spirited for the rest of that day. The lady redialed Kim's number after learning that she was yelling at the wrong person. She told Kim that her husband was having an affair with a lady called Kim, who called earlier that day and exchanged some bitter words with her.

The time for the annual interim evaluation had arrived. The director passed out a memo to all unit supervisors to prepare and conduct the evaluation of their unit staff. Kim had never done the employee evaluation before and didn't like to consult her peers of what was required for the evaluation processes. She consulted Amy and Vicky, to see if they had any idea of how to evaluate staff or simply provide their previous evaluation form to help her prepare their evaluation.

She first went to Vicky. "Vicky, I'm in the process of preparing your interim evaluation. I don't want to be hard on some of you. That is why I'd like you to show me how the scores from your previous evaluations look, if you don't mind?" she said in a smart way to convince Vicky.

"Of course I do mind. These are confidential reports. I rather suggest you locate the blank form in the default library."

"Why do I have to go that far if you could just hand me yours? I'll take it from there." Kim didn't even know how to access the default library. She wanted an easy fix, a filled-out form she would be able to make some minor changes to and put her signature on it.

"I'm sorry, Kim. I don't think I will be of any help to you right now."

Kim left Vicky's cubicle without further insistence. She declined to ask Amy, but planned to talk to Katie later that evening when she got out of work.

Kim went to Katie's apartment later that evening and found her still in the bathroom. Her boyfriend opened the door and welcomed Kim into the house.

"I'm Devon." He extended his hand for greetings.

Kim's hand met his halfway, and they shook hands. "I'm Kim, Katie's friend."

"Welcome, Kim. I came from D.C. this morning for a one-week business trip," said Devon with some sort of pride.

"Welcome to our state. How's Washington?" She was excited to meet a man from Washington, D.C.

"Pretty busy there."

"What do you do there?" Kim was a curiosity seeker and loved to dig even into affairs that were not of her concern.

"We make laws," Devon proudly said.

"Wow! That sounds wonderful."

Katie joined Devon and Kim in the living room.

"Hi, Kim." She walked back to take a seat close to her boyfriend.

"Honey, this is my friend, Kim."

"We have just introduced ourselves while you were away, but thanks for that," Devon responded.

"Sure we did. He's such a wonderful gentleman," said Kim.

"He is my babe. Congressman Dee. I'm sure you never met him before."

"No, we never met before," said Kim.

Devon nodded his head in response. Katie excused herself and left for the kitchen to prepare dinner. Devon and Kim were in the living room and silently stared at each other. Katie had no idea what Kim was about to do behind her back. Kim took off her jacket under the pretext that she was feeling hot, only to draw Devon's attention by revealing those adoring boobs. She asked Devon. "Is it okay with you if I remain without the jacket." I feel terribly hot, and I don't even know why."

Devon expressed no concern. "You are most welcome." He said. She looked right into his eyes, then asked further. "Are there more handsome young lawmakers like you in Washington?"

In response, he said. "There are many out there than I can count." Kim then asked for Devon's office phone number, which Devon happily gave her. At that point, Katie came back and asked the two to join in and have dinner.

"What happened? Are you feeling that hot even under the normal room temperature?" asked Katie.

"Very hot. I have been feeling like this ever since," said Kim.

Katie knew Kim was a cold-blooded animal who kept her jacket on all day, even under the summer heat. For Kim to feel hot in the apartment with a seventy-degree temperature was ridiculous. Kim had issues with running after her friends' boyfriends. That last one was her desperate attempt to catch the big fish. She never took her eyes off Devon, even at the dinner table. Devon never paid close attention to her, but talked to Katie most of the time.

Katie was rather irritated with some of the comments Kim made and came up with a plan to force her to leave.

She reluctantly said, "Kim, I'm afraid we can't hang out tonight. Dee has an important function we have to attend tonight. Perhaps we will hang out next week."

"That's fine. I'm actually about to leave." She put on her jacket and walked toward the door, looking disappointed. "I would like to meet your boyfriend again before he leaves. Could we arrange for that? Perhaps we could go out for dinner together." She stood there for a while and waited for Katie to respond.

"Sure. I'll come up with the date." Katie just wanted her to leave and nothing else.

Kim left the apartment and headed straight for home to nurse her loneliness.

The due date for the interim evaluation was pushed back by one week. Kim had not yet done the evaluation for her employees. She was counting on Katie for help, but never heard from her since they last met. Katie was mad at Kim after Devon told her what Kim did when she was preparing dinner. Kim tried to reach her by phone, but the calls went unanswered.

Kim was at the point of panic. She didn't know what to do next week if she wasn't done with the evaluation. She sought help from some of her friends in the department, and she got one to match. The friend, a supervisor for Child Adoption Unit, had no idea of what her unit did. She didn't know a single policy on child adoption and had looked upon foster parents as abusers whose actions were legalized by laws that were supposed to protect the very lives of the endangered children.

"How far have you gone with the evaluation process of your employees?" asked Kim.

"I haven't started that yet. I was kinda busy revising and rewriting adoption policies."

"Wow! That must be interesting."

"Interesting indeed. The old policies are messy, and I'm trying to rewrite some new ones that would tighten the children adoption practices in this state. I believe that would reduce the exploitation of disadvantaged children by their adopted parents."

"That's impressive. You are a genius, but how long will that take you to complete?"

"At least a year if I work on it fast enough."

The friend had little problem conning Kim as if she had all that knowledge to overhaul the child adoption policies of the department. She impressed Kim to an extent of even misleading her into assigning poor ratings for her employees.

"When are you gonna do your evaluation?" Kim asked.

"Today if I feel like it. It's very simple."

"How's that? I'm sorry. I never did it before." Kim was direct this time. She was desperate and needed immediate help.

"Just get in there and fill out the form. Remember, a score of five points for friends and a score of three or less points for the rest."

"Are you serious?"

"Why did you ask if you feel like I'm not?"

Kim was ready to take whatever was offered to her at the time. "Thank you so much for the help. I'll be back if I need further assistance." Kim left her friend's office armed with the wrong tools for her to be devastating in the evaluation.

Before she could even start, she called her friend again. "Hey, friend. This is Kim again."

"Yes, Kim, how can I help you?"

"I tried to locate the interim evaluation form, but, for some reasons, I couldn't." Kim lied. She didn't even know where to look for the interim evaluation forms.

Her friend thought that giving Kim some of the instructions by phone was just a waste of time. She left her cubicle. Within minutes, she was at Kim's cubicle.

"Where did you search for the forms?"

Kim started fumbling. "It was here on this site. No, not here. Probably the next one." She was all over the Internet.

The friend knew Kim was in real trouble and technologically challenged. "Step aside. Let me do the search." After few clicks, she pulled up the evaluation form. "This is where you need to go."

"Wow! That was fast. Thank you for the help. I don't know how I would have gotten it without your help."

"We need each other in times like this. This is DCS, remember?" She got up from the chair.

"I certainly do, but sometimes confused though."

"That's even better. We thrive well in state of confusion, don't we?"

That was precisely right. Both she and Kim did manage by crisis, and steering a state of confusion was their virtue. They both suffered from managerial deficiency syndrome, a rare malignant tumor associated with aggressive behavior commonly identified with females who are allergic to men.

Kim printed the forms and then got ready to evaluate her employees. She started with Amy and gave her all the score of five. Vicky was given six scores of five and one score of three for refusing to accompany her on lunch. Steve got one score of four and six scores of three. Reggie and Tina got identical scores, all threes. Two days later, Kim went and showed the draft to her friend, the architect of the evaluation scores for comments.

"Thank God. I've finally gotten hold of the evaluations." She handed the evaluations over to her friend.

"They look good, but you need to provide comments to support your decision."

"What comments? These scores are self-explanatory. A score of five is for excellent, four is for very good, and three is for average. Besides, I sympathized enough not to give some of the idiots the scores of twos and super ones," Kim said proudly.

Her friend shook her head in disbelief. She couldn't imagine Kim was so dumb to an extent of taking advice from someone like her. "You got that right, girl." The friend went through all the forms one by one. The third form was Steve's evaluation. "Who's this one?"

"He's Steve, my lead worker."

"Why did you give him all these happy threes and one miserable four?"

"Don't you remember the rules you spelled out two days ago?" She played by the rules of the lips.

Her friend never believed that Kim had that many enemies within her unit. "Is he cute?"

"Adorable. Believe me. I don't even know why I'm doing this." She immediately changed her perception. "But yes. He's mean, and he deserved that." She pointed at the poor scores she assigned to Steve.

"Can't you turn the wheels around?"

"You mean the wheels of fortune?"

"Exactly right. It might work for you."

"Work for me! Purr, I belong to Washington, D.C." She now focused her intention on getting Devon away from Katie at any cost.

"That's a very narrow path, like the way to heaven."

"That's not for me. I have wings, and I can fly. I have tentacles long enough to grab the hidden treasures from beneath the ocean." That was a self-promotion of the first degree for someone like Kim who was supposed to put herself together before her wild assumptions.

"Can you show me who this Steve is?"

"What are you gonna do with him?"

"Gettin' to know him. We all work in DCS, don't we?"

"Yes, we all do." Kim halted.

She felt jealous as if her friend was getting an easy access to Steve at her expense. Perhaps she had a sort of silent love for him, but his unresponsive nature might have possibly triggered some sort of anger that turned into undeclared hatred and revenge.

"Do you have any problem with that?" The friend looked right into Kim's eyes.

"No! Not at all. I'll be more than happy to show him to you one day."

She left and went back to her office. She quickly erased the score of four from the evaluation form and left Steve with all threes.

"That's for being cute in the eyes of ladies. You selfish, handsome idiot!" she said to herself.

A day before the deadline for submitting the interim evaluations to the director, Kim conducted one-on-one conferences with her unit staff to review the evaluation and have them sign the final forms for the director's review. She started with Amy and then Vicky, who gladly signed the forms and walked out with joy. Steve, Reggie, and Tina contested the evaluation and refused to sign their evaluation forms.

"I have been nice for offering you the best I could, and you're still not satisfied. What are you gonna do if I gave you the scores you really deserve?"

"I don't deserve that kind of mistreatment from you, Kim," Steve protested.

"Whatever. Tell me what you want. Do you want five-point scores? I don't think so," she responded arrogantly.

"Are we done with the review?" Steve was utterly disappointed with his scores. He felt he deserved better scores than what Kim had assigned.

"Pretty much so, except for your signature." She placed the forms flat on the table and pushed them toward Steve.

"I'm not gonna sign that. I'm sorry." Steve grabbed the forms from the table and tossed it back to Kim.

"With or without your signature, it's a done deal."

Seconds later, Steve walked out of the conference room. Kim stood up and watched as he closed the door behind him. Kim got annoyed. She threw the evaluation forms in air, and the papers quickly scattered throughout the room. A knock at the door got her even more nervous. She tried to pick up the papers before allowing Reggie to come in, but it was too late. Reggie went ahead, cranked the door open, and walked in. Kim dived under the table to recover some of the papers. She cursed repeatedly after banging her head hard against the metal frame underneath the table. Her head was stuck between the closely packed conference chairs, and she desperately struggled to free herself.

Reggie sat down and quietly watched Kim on her belly, undulating with papers in hand. She wished she could level the table on her to cause maximum pain. Kim finally set herself free and recovered all the forms. She set them on the table and straightened her skirt and blouse.

She looked at Reggie with a bitter dislike. "Did I ask you to come in after you knocked the door?"

"But you were somersaulting under the table. Besides, my appointment time was up."

"Time is subject to change."

"But you never changed the appointment time, did you?"

"Of course not, but I was about to."

"Who's to blame for that?"

"Yourself, for not giving me enough time to get things together." Kim looked distressed.

She knew very well that Reggie was even worse than Steve was. She wanted to postpone her review, but the due date was the next day. She wouldn't meet the deadline if she postponed the conference. She sat down and started searching for Reggie's evaluation forms from among the disorderly pile of the clumsy papers. She finally found all three pages and assembled them together.

"I was with Steve a while ago, and he didn't want to sign the forms." She looked at Reggie. "What I want from you is just your signature on the last page of the forms. Then we are done. I will set you free, and you can go for an early lunch right from here and come back after a good one-and-a-half hours with my approval." She handed the signature page to Reggie and retained the first two pages.

"This page says signature of the employee and date. How could I know if it's intended for me or someone else?" Reggie asked.

"Because I know it's intended for you. That's why I want you to sign."

"Are you kidding me?" Reggie grew annoyed. "How do you expect me to sign without reading the content of the review?" She flung the sheet back to Kim and walked away cursing. "Come kiss my ass, bitch."

"Who are you calling bitch, you moron?" Kim yelled.

But Reggie never looked back. She walked out and banged the door really hard after her. Kim had created monsters out of her own employees who never had issues with their previous supervisors. She still had Tina to deal with. Kim knew she had more enemies than friends in the unit. She called Tina on her office phone because she wanted to reschedule the conference for early morning the next day. But it was too late. Tina was just by the door outside the conference room, waiting for her time to come up. Steve and Reggie had already briefed her, and she was going to add her name to the list of Kim's critics, if not enemies. She knocked hard twice.

"Come in," Kim asked her.

"I just called you, but you never picked up my call. Why?"

"Because I wasn't there to answer your call."

"Were you away from your office without prior permission from your supervisor?"

"The supervisor scheduled me for a conference. That doesn't require further permission." She looked at Kim to see what she had to say.

But Kim never replied back. She wanted to at least succeed in her last effort. "Can we put off our conference for tomorrow morning?"

"Not really. You know I requested for a day off tomorrow."

Kim delved into her bag for the black book and immediately pulled it out, only to confirm she had indeed approved the day off.

"Shit! I can't believe this." Kim was already disappointed, and her luck seemed to have slipped away.

After few encounters with Tina, Kim gave up and let her go without further argument. Kim packed the forms and left the conference room looking terrible. She never went for lunch that day, but got permission to leave early instead.

Home wasn't a resting place for Kim either. Her boyfriend had deserted her two years earlier, and he was happily married to his college sweetheart. Since then, Kim had acted crazy. Her attempts for a new boyfriend never succeeded, partly due to her unfaithful affairs with other men. Her last promotion was even dubious, and she now felt like even quitting the supervisory position in exchange for a permanent boyfriend if one came her way. She wanted to gamble on her chances with Devon, if she could sway him away from Katie. And that would be like extracting blood out of stone, but not impossible to try anyway.

The following morning, Kim reported to the office earlier than usual. She wanted to blackmail and find out who among the three would report late to work even by a minute. She also planned to instigate chaos between Steve and Vicky or Amy by trying to get into his computer and sending out a derogatory message. She did get on to his computer that morning, but failed to log in to his e-mail. She tried three times. She was finally kicked out and referred to the administrator for a password reset.

Steve, Reggie, and Tina arrived in the office ahead of time. Kim told them not to log on to their computers until seven o'clock, and they did wait for that time to log on. Steve tried to open his e-mail, but failed. He immediately informed Kim about the problem.

"You probably have a virus on your computer," Kim said.

"Let's try to talk sense here. This is a government computer, and antivirus software protects it."

"I'm busy. Call tech support, and don't call me again for the same issue. Do you understand?"

Steve called tech support. A technician told him someone tried to access his e-mail account at sixty thirty and was locked out after three attempts. Steve went with that report to the director, and she also confirmed that from the technician. The director called an emergency meeting to address the issue. She first met with Kim separately to investigate if she had anything to do with Steve's computer.

"I checked his port to investigate if he still has porn pictures or visited porn Web sites."

"Did you obtain any consent from him to log on to his computer?"

"No, ma'am. I got in as the supervisor, and I guess I have the right to do so."

"Who granted you those powers to do so?"

"That's what all the supervisors do."

"Not exactly. That's a violation of one's privacy, and you could be charged for that."

Kim was quiet. She even denied attempting to get into Steve's e-mail account. She said Steve left his computer open overnight, and that was why she was able to check the port. They had a long meeting. At the end, the director gave her a verbal warning about never again interfering with her employees' computers. She was also asked to hand in her evaluation forms immediately after the meeting.

Kim went to her office, hurriedly packed the evaluation forms in an envelope, and rushed them to the director's office, but the director wasn't there. Kim was relieved. At least for now she could breathe easy. She left the envelope on the director's desk and dashed out. Then she called the director to say she had to leave for the hospital to attend to someone who had a car accident. Kim took her multipurpose bag from the drawer and then quickly disappeared to avoid the director summoning her again that day.

The director came to Kim's office minutes later to ask about the nature of the accident and if she needed some extra time off. Her message and urgent departure even worried the director. Kim committed a serious scam just to avoid meeting the director over the blunder she had made in the evaluation reports. The lack of knowledge had given way to self-destruction and deception. She not only feared the director, but her subordinates as well. She went home and disconnected the phone line. Then she turned off the cell phone as well. She needed no calls of any nature that whole day. She called the director to let her know she wouldn't be in the office that Friday.

It was easy to set on fire, but difficult to put it off. That was what Kim went through. She tried to recollect her memories to figure out what really went wrong when she decided to get onto Steve's computer and why wasn't she having a working relationship with her own employees. She came to the wrong conclusion again.

"Steve doesn't respect me because I'm a female," she said to herself. "Okay, Steve, let's see who will be the winner in this game. I know you're an ass kisser, but I am gonna tell you what I am capable of doing."

She continued to talk to herself for a lengthy amount of time. At times, she got very emotional and threw herself against the wall, the bed, and the couch. Or she buried her tear-soaked face into the pillow as if hiding from the shame befalling her. She remained home all day Friday. There were no phone calls and no knocks at the door. It was herself alone. Everything around her looked transient, and she felt like her life was ending. She had eaten nothing since the previous day, and she already felt weak and depressed.

Kim turned on her cell phone late that night and connected the home phone line as well. A half hour later, her cell phone rang. Amy was calling to find out how she was dealing with the news of the car accident.

"Hello, hello? This is me, Amy."

"Hi, Amy. I'm glad you called. I have been having a hard time since yesterday. Can I call you back after five minutes, please?"

"That will be fine. I will be on standby for your call." Amy hung up and then quickly connected to continue with a conversation with Vicky.

"Hello, sunshine. What's the news?" asked Vicky.

"Hello, girlfriend. I'm back again as promised." She was excited for getting back with Vicky.

"What have you to tell me, girl?"

"She finally picked up my phone for the first time since yesterday. Can you imagine that?" Amy said with some concern.

"Is the relative dead? I hope not." Vicky was a little worried. She felt sorry for what Kim might be going through.

"She promised to call me back, and I will fill you in once I talk to her." Someone was trying to call her cell phone. She checked the incoming call, and it was Kim's number. "I'll call you back in a while. Kim is calling."

She put Kim through. "Hello, Kim. Sorry. I was on line with Vicky."

"That's fine. How are you girls doing?"

"We're doing fine. And you?"

"I'm feeling weak and tired." She answered in a faint voice, like someone who had just woken from sleep.

"I know. Dealing with such situations isn't all that easy. How's the condition of the person who was in the car accident?"

Kim hesitated for a while. "That's a long story, Amy. I don't really know where to start."

Her statement made Amy even more worried. She assumed the person had actually passed away or was in a coma at best. She, however, composed herself. "I'm so sorry for your loss. How old was the deceased?"

Amy actually meant to ask if the person involved in the car accident was a male or female. She expected to get that answer from Kim, who remained silent. Kim tried to come up with an answer for Amy, but that took her forever.

"Are you all right, ma'am?" Amy asked.

But there was still no answer. Kim was still on the line, and Amy could hear her movements.

"Okay, Kim, I'm gonna come there with Vicky right out. Expect us in a half hour."

Amy hung up with Kim and dialed Vicky's number right away.

"Hello, dear. What's going on?" asked Vicky.

"Please come to my apartment. Hurry up. We need to go to Kim right away."

Amy and Vicky were three blocks apart. Ten minutes later, Vicky joined her on their way to Kim's apartment. They knocked at her door. She opened it and led them to the large living room. Kim spent half of her income on rent. She lived out loud. One couldn't understand why on earth a single woman like her should rent a three-bedroom apartment.

"I was very worried when you couldn't talk to me on phone. Is everything all right?" asked Amy.

Kim lifted her head. "Thanks to both of you for coming." She got up from where she was seated and then hugged them both before settling down beside Amy.

"We understand how hard it is to be alone at this moment. Take courage. We will be here to grieve with you," said Vicky.

At that moment, Kim decided to be more forthcoming. "I am sorry to put you all through this." Amy and Vicky waited anxiously for every word. "I was upset that day, and I wanted to get out of the office as quickly as possible. That was why I had to frame that accident as the only possible reason to leave the office." She looked down and started sobbing.

"Why do you do that to yourself? That's completely unacceptable, especially with the director now involved in sending out e-mails for contributions and a sympathy card." Amy was very upset. She would have left Kim's apartment and went back home if she wasn't in Vicky's company.

"Yes, we now know a damage has been caused. How are you gonna fix that come Monday when all employees in the department come to offer you their sympathies? How about the get-well card and the contribution for flowers and fruit basket?" Vicky shrugged and signaled to Amy that they could leave.

But Amy objected. "You can't leave without me. We came here to keep her company. Isn't it?" She said. Vicky nodded her head in acceptance.

"I'm defenseless and vulnerable to any kind of criticisms. I blame myself for making stupid decisions, and I deeply regret that," said Kim.

Amy came up with a brighter suggestion. "You need to act immediately once you get to the office on Monday. First, you need to send an e-mail to everyone and thank them for their support, but don't take the contributions. You need to clarify in the message that the rumor was not true. It was the relative of your former boyfriend they tried to reach, but were not able to. That was why they called your number. Let the contribution money be kept in the revolving funds for future use."

"Wow! That is absolutely fabulous. I feel much better already," said Kim.

Her main worry was what to say to the director the coming Monday. With that plan in place, Kim would be able to face the director with fewer concerns. At least for now, she seemed to have secured some comrades in crime.

One should never let subordinates know about areas of weakness. Kim let Amy and Vicky know that, and she had even accepted the lies that Amy coined for a deceptive argument without analyzing the future implications that may come to bear on her. Amy and Vicky became indispensable for her, and she would readily dance at their tunes to survive in her very position of supervisor. That would be a bitter pill for her to swallow, but she got herself into it. She had to carry her own cross.

Vicky and Amy stayed at Kim's apartment until late that night. They had some pizza for dinner and watched some movies as their sorrow turned into a joyful event. Kim was pleased for the two confidantes rescuing her. Kim accompanied them to the parking when they decided to leave. Then she went back into the room as Vicky and Amy got into the car and left for the night.

"What do you think of all the mess she made?" asked Vicky.

"I'm afraid she won't come out of it clean." Amy lowered her speed to pay attention to their conversation.

"There are times when you might not feel like helping people who can't help themselves, isn't it?" Vicky asked.

"You're right. I feel guilty already for even making such a suggestion. It seems I have implicated myself into this mess."

"Big time, honey. You think I was stupid for keeping a low profile."

"Why are you telling me now? You should have warned me there and then."

"Okay, please drive. See, you almost missed to turn right."

Amy tried to negotiate a sharp right turn. She went over the curb and landed back into the road with a loud bang.

"Gosh, I'm having a very bad time," she complained as they approached Vicky's apartment.

She came to a stop right at Vicky's doorway and missed a light pole by some inches.

"Thanks, Amy. Take everything easy for now. We'll go over those things tomorrow morning. Good-bye!" Vicky then went toward the door.

Amy reversed the car and soon disappeared into the dark as she headed for home.

Monday came too soon for many who wished to stay home for one extra day. Kim would have taken it off if she hadn't taken off Friday. She arrived in the office close to seven o'clock and remained in her office to send the e-mail for the departmental staff. She explained everything, as Amy had planned. She also added some lines of apology to those who were mislead by her information. She, however, left out Steve, Reggie, and Tina in her e-mail.

The director called her early that morning. She also noticed that Kim had eliminated the names of Steve, Tina, and Reggie from the email, consistent with her evaluation reports where all three were given the scores of three or lower, even in the areas of their best performances like punctuality and time management, follow-up and documentation, and much more. Kim joined the director in the conference room for the meeting that lasted well beyond the scheduled time. The director did most of the talking. Kim was answering most of the time.

"Who gave you that awful information about the accident?" the director asked.

Kim was already nervous. "My former boyfriend's reckless brother did."

"Why did he do that? He knew very well that his brother is no longer with you?"

"I have no idea. He called from Idaho, where he's lived for the last four years."

"That was unfortunate, but I'm glad things worked out well on your part."

"Yes, ma'am. I'm kinda relieved now."

"Are you sure you don't want the contributions and the card anymore?"

"No, ma'am. I better do without. Let the contribution money be placed into the revolving fund."

"All right, let's move to our next topic." The director pulled out the copy of the e-mail Kim sent earlier that morning. "Why didn't you copy three of your employees in your e-mail?" She looked directly into Kim's eyes.

"Because I planned to talk to them in person this morning."

"Have you informed them about that?"

"Not yet. I was about to do so when I received your message and immediately left for this meeting." Kim seemed to have answers for every question that the director asked.

"Did you meet with all the employees during the review?" The director kept grilling Kim with question after question, but she was no match to Kim.

"Yes, I did. Some were upset with the scores and refused to sign their evaluation forms. I refer to that insubordination."

The director went through Steve's evaluation form and once again noticed all the scores of three were given for every standard and nothing else. "Are you sure you meant to assign these scores for him and the other two?"

"Seriously, yes. Those were the best scores I could give them at the time of my review. The score of two points would have actually been a possibility after they refused to sign their review forms." Kim was very adamant. She wasn't even aware of whom she was talking to.

The director was in total disbelief. "Why can't you revise some of the scores and come up with something acceptable for you and the three staff?"

"If you ordered me to do so, ma'am." She loosened a bit to accommodate the director's suggestion.

"I don't give orders to question your decision, but I offer suggestions that would help you improve your relations with the staff, am I right?"

"Sure you are."

Kim brought up the behavioral issues, citing that Tina and Reggie walked away from their individual conferences. She said that Steve actually attempted to befriend her, but she warned him, as she considered it was inappropriate, and turned him down.

"Why didn't you bring that to my attention from before?"

Kim wasted no time in answering the question. "Because you trusted him more than me." Kim bluntly threw it into the director's face.

"Are you trying to accuse me of favoring Steve over you? Please, we don't need to go the wrong way when we try to get things right."

"Sorry, ma'am. That's how I feel. I may be wrong, but I'd better bring it up." Kim brought out all the defense mechanisms to battle the raging cold war with the director. She was determined to defend every decision she made and even lie when the situation warranted.

They never reached a concrete solution after their lengthy discussion. The director asked her to revise the review forms and submit the signed copies to her within three days. She was also instructed to call a meeting to address some of the fundamental issues in her unit. Kim agreed to comply with the directives. The director left for another meeting. Kim went back to her office and then immediately sent an e-mail for an urgent meeting she scheduled for the next day and copied the director.

Kim assembled her staff for an early-morning meeting as planned, and the director joined them within minutes after they got into the conference room.

"I am glad you're all here for this meeting, and I would like to thank the director for joining us as we have some serious issues to discuss." Kim said. Everybody was attentive. "We have three topics on the agenda to discuss, and I would like each one of you to offer your opinions and suggestions, as we need to get to the bottom of these issues."

"The first topic is the lack of discipline in this unit. By this, I mean the three of you." She pointed at Steve, Reggie, and Tina. "I have been observing your activities and conduct from the first day I took over this unit, and nothing seems to have changed as far as your behaviors are concerned. I tried everything to make the cooperation between you and me work, but always meet stiff resistance from you folks. Vicky, Amy, and I get along quite well because they appreciate all the good things I do for this unit, am I right?"

The room was virtually quiet, and that irritated Kim even more.

"Am I talking to myself here? Amy and Vicky, what is your opinion on what I have just said?"

She wanted to induce the two into submission, but there was no response from them yet. They knew very well that Kim had credibility issues. Siding with her in the presence of the director would cast doubt on their own judgments.

"Vicky, speak up. Am I right or not?" said Kim.

Vicky shrugged and said in low voice, "I don't know. Please leave me alone."

Everyone laughed out loud.

"Whatever. I have done my best to pull this unit together, and y'all know that well." She then started talking about Steve being disrespectful to her. She accused him of inciting Reggie and Tina against her, Amy, and Vicky. "How do you expect to get higher scores in your evaluation if you haven't shown respect to someone with whom your future career lies?" She raised her personalized pen. "Your fate lies here."

The director intervened. "We are not here to discuss personal grudges. Let's stick to the topics and nothing more."

"I'm not being mean. If I were, believe me, some of you would have been on the streets by now." She slipped back to personal attacks.

The director reprimanded her this time. "Do we have some personality issues here? And if we do, I want it to stop right now."

"Fair enough," said a voice from behind the scene.

"Speak out loud, you coward," groaned Kim, looking eccentric this time.

Reggie stuck out her tongue.

Kim went ballistic. "Have y'all seen what she did to me?" Kim exploded defiantly, but, unfortunately, only Kim saw Reggie do that.

"Who did what to you, Kim?" Tina jumped in.

"Shut your big mouth, bitch. I'm not talking to you in the first place." Kim swung at Tina momentarily.

"Stop calling names. That's very unprofessional," said the director.

"A despicable street girl. That's what she is!" Reggie was very temperamental and probably restrained herself because of the director's presence.

Her physique alone was very compelling, and Kim wouldn't afford to have that used on her. She looked at the director and expected her to interfere, but the director remained silent.

"Why am I the only one being rebuked while others throw insults against me?" Kim complained.

Kim found herself fighting a lone war. Her lieutenants, Amy and Vicky, remained at bay and watched the show. She quickly moved to the second topic on the agenda as a divergent and read out angrily.

"Job assignments for next month."

The director cautioned her. "Did you just say reassignments?"

Kim looked in her direction. "Yes, ma'am. I have redesigned assignments for the staff that I would like to see implemented in the coming months."

"Let me ask you one more time. Have you read the guidelines for the job assignments for your unit?"

"Not yet. I planned to read it during my free time," she said proudly.

"If I can remember correctly, the policy stipulates that job assignments in your unit are carried out every six months and prior to consultation with the director. Have I been made aware of this?"

Kim went nuts. "This is more complicated than I thought. Never mind the girls and him over there." She looked at Steve. "I'll let you continue with your current assignments until we sort out things with the director." She quickly jumped to the third topic as the director reminded her of the time left. "We are running out of our scheduled time. I believe this last topic won't take us long to wrap up the meeting." She paused. "Vicky and Amy are awarded with special recognition as employees of the month for their outstanding performances in our unit. Congratulations to both of you. I and the director will arrange to take you out for a special treat at Laguna Peak Restaurant."

Steve and Reggie clapped hard and congratulated the two for the recognition they didn't really deserve. Vicky felt embarrassed for being drawn into Kim's bizarre game. Amy didn't care as long as the director said nothing about Kim's recklessness. She, however, didn't appreciate the idea of the special treat. Kim's unprecedented behavior, especially her demise and lack of rational judgment, appalled the director. She excused herself and left the conference room for other business.

Kim quickly declared the meeting over and then said. "I would like to meet with you Steve, Reggie, and Tina tomorrow morning so you could sign the evaluation forms.

"Do you want to meet with us as a group or individually?" Reggie asked

"Individually of course." Kim responded promptly.

"Just sent us the schedule for the meetings and we will be there," said Tina.

Sure, I will once I get to my office." She e-mailed the schedule immediately to avoid further confrontation with the group.

Kim took the evaluation forms home that evening and altered the scores to fives and fours to appease the director. She also knew that was her last chance to come out clean, a compromise she wouldn't afford to lose.

She met with Steve. While there, she bent over his desk and revealed her boobs that hung loose in the blouse. Steve turned away his head to avoid staring at them.

"You look like a rapist. Haven't you seen a beautiful body like this before?" she said provocatively.

"If I were, I still wouldn't rape someone like you. I would go for something better and real."

Steve was ready for confrontation that morning, and he had to give her maximum pain and embarrassment she deserved. His remark took Kim off balance.

She straightened up and looked at him straight in the eyes. "I'm doing you a big favor, you loser. Just sign the papers. I'll be back once I'm done with the director. Save your words for now."

She left and walked forcefully as if ordered to dig holes in the carpet with her pointed high heel shoes. She met with Reggie and then Tina. They also signed the revised version of the forms before Kim could take them to the director for final endorsement. Kim felt like a real loser, but who cared. As one of her friends remarked, she still had her job.

Chapter Four

Six Months Later

Kim had lost a significant amount of weight in her struggle to stay afloat. She also managed to make new enemies across the department, and that greatly limited her movement parameters. She no longer went to the break room for lunch, and she repealed the rule that forbid eating lunch in the office. Her unruly behavior, however, remained intact. Steve and Reggie were her main concerns, and she feared them most. She avoided riding in an elevator with Reggie when other people were not around. She feared that Reggie might strangle her in the elevator and walk away without anyone knowing.

That illusion gave way to hatred and then self-isolation. Kim no longer wanted to call for regular unit meetings. She even started escaping departmental meetings that the director chaired. The world was slipping away beneath her feet. No one ever stepped forward in her rescue. Kim sometimes forgot her routine makeup. At one occasion, she even put on a different pair of shoes until Tina realized it and sympathetically reminded her of what she had on her feet. Tina advised her to get permission and go home. That was the first time Kim took advice from someone she considered an enemy. She packed her stuff in the bag and left for the day.

The hidden scam of the accident surfaced after three months when Kim accidentally told her friend about the lie she framed, "Do you remember the incident when I stayed home for two days?"

Not really, could you tell me what happened?" The friend asked

"There was no accident, I framed it up just to escape from workplace, I would have gotten into real trouble if it weren't for Vicky and Amy who came up with a rescue plan." She said.

"Girl, I was even pissed off and couldn't figure out what to do," she added.

"That was stupid in the first place. You should have kept that to yourself for the rest of life," her friend said.

Kim prepared to explain the rest of the story. "I got emotional and totally upset. I tried to walk away from the workplace, but had no good reason to excuse myself." She checked if the friend was listening. "I made up the accident story to free myself from there. I felt belittled and humiliated."

"Then what? Only to expose your lies to your own workers. That wasn't fun at all." Her friend kept criticizing Kim for making wrong choices.

Kim sat quietly and listened. She seemed more awful than Kim herself. At one point, she encouraged Kim to continue chasing after Devon. "Katie doesn't own men. They are out there for every woman who could be attractive to them. Katie and Devon are just friends. I mean he hasn't made any commitment to her. My piece of advice is that you should put your friendship with Katie on hold and go after him. If you need any help, just let me know. I'm gonna get you to where you wanna be."

Kim dipped a hand into her handbag and drew out the black book, her diary. "Here's his phone number. He gave it to me secretly when we met at Katie's apartment."

She lied. Devon never gave the number voluntarily. She had asked for it with intent to lure him away from Katie.

"I told you. He liked a fresh look, not those wrinkled and pimple-ridden faces like hers. Listen, baby girl. He is my homey. I will find out when he will be in the town from his aunt who lives right here. We will arrange to meet him at his aunt's house. Do you have any objection to that?"

"Nothing better than what you have just said." Kim liked the idea and looked forward to meeting Devon anytime he showed up in town.

"Anything else?" her friend asked.

"I don't think so. We better take care of this Devon business once and for all. I can't rest without getting him in my life."

"Rest assured, baby girl, but never underestimate the powers of your own friend."

"I know you are everything to me, and I put my entire life into your hands." Kim looked convinced and thought she was in good hands.

Unfortunately, Kim not only did mess with someone untrustworthy, but she hooked up with a real con girl who fed her friends with misleading information. Kim's friendship with Katie would soon take a downhill turn and never recover for many years.

Kim tried to call Devon's phone number many times without a success. Every time she called, the secretary told her the congressman was in a meeting. She asked Kim if she would like to leave a message.

Kim would say, "No, thank you." Then she would hang up the phone.

Kim kept trying until one late evening when she got through. They talked briefly. Devon gave her another phone number to call only at late hours when he got home. Now Kim saw the light coming from the end of the tunnel, even without her friend's involvement.

Devon secretly gave Kim his new cell phone number, which Katie herself didn't have and wouldn't ever have as Devon secretly transited from her into Kim's world. Kim was young and beautiful, but very lousy, too. That was all what one needed to get to understand her better. Kim would keep pumping Devon over the phone for the next three months or so and sometimes send pictures of her from the phone. Her cell phone screen went blurred from those repeated kisses.

"Who elected this Devon to be the peoples' representative in Washington?" a customer asked after learning about his swindling love affairs with women.

"The American people did. Any problem with that?" The gas station manager responded.

"No, I am just curious."

"I was from the beginning, but later learned out how he maneuvered his way into the public office."

"How was that? I'm not from here and probably don't understand the politics of the area."

"The front-runner in the election disappeared two days before the election and turned up dead on the very day of the election."

"Very sad. Who did that to him? Don't tell me he did it."

"No. I won't even go that far. His wife did it after learning of his secret love affair with another Hollywood star." He paused a little. "Devon became a unanimous candidate, walking into the public office unchallenged."

"God forbid. I wish he lived."

"What difference would it make? He would be another side of the same coin. Do you understand what I mean?"

"Sure I did. Womanizers, aren't they?"

"Absolutely right. The kind of problems associated with young politicians."

They cut the discussion short as another customer walked into the store.

Kim kept pumping on Devon day in and day out until she persuaded him to come down and meet her in person. Her wish was granted when the House was on recess for two weeks, and Devon decided to spend it in his hometown. He took a cab from the airport straight to where Kim worked. He checked at the reception and was directed to Kim's floor.

"Excuse me, ladies. I'm looking for Ms. Kim," Devon asked the secretary.

She responded immediately, "Two cubicles on your left, sir."

"Thanks," Devon said.

The secretary paid less attention, but let him take care of the rest. "That is fine. Have a nice day, sir."

Devon left to locate Kim's office. Kim was busy working on her computer. She lifted up her head and immediately saw the man of her dreams, a tall and well-groomed man in a pleasant suit, smiling and staring at her. She jumped from her seat and tightly held onto his neck. Then she started kissing him again and again until her lips wore thin. She slowly loosened her arms to let his neck go. She held him by the hand and led him away from her office and into the elevator bound to the ground level, where they sat in the lobby and conversed at length. Kim went back upstairs to the eighth floor and got permission to go home. She rushed back downstairs to meet her man, and they left for home.

After leaving Devon at home, Kim went back to the office to request two days of vacation. The director approved it that same day. She told Vicky and Amy she planned to go out of town with her fiancé and wouldn't be back until Monday morning. She left the office early that Wednesday to join her new boyfriend at her apartment. They appeared to be ideal for one another, given their deceptive lifestyles. Kim was, however, different this time. She wanted a partner for the rest of her life. If Devon could offer her one, then that would be it. She wanted to settle down and have children of her own. In the coming days and months, she would press Devon to make her a commitment for marriage, which he reluctantly did by getting her an expensive engagement diamond ring.

Katie never heard from Devon after he deviated his attention to Kim. He came to town twice and never bothered to call or approach Katie to let her know he had broken up with her. Katie was left to dig his actions all by herself and with some little help from Miki, who had advised Kim to go after Devon. Miki had a personal misunderstanding over money. She desperately needed Katie to pay her past due on apartment rent after losing her job, but Katie turned her down. Kim helped her with some money to pay the rent. That was why she worked hard for Katie's downfall. The relationship between Kim and Devon continued to flourish and got even stronger as Devon finally dumped Katie and got engaged to Kim.

The following week after their engagement, the news was on everyone's lips. Kim spread the news like wildfire throughout the department and friends everywhere. Steve and his co-workers learned from the director, who sent an e-mail congratulating Kim for the engagement and wished her the best of life in their future. The elegant diamond ring on Kim's finger further reinforced the reality that she was indeed on her way to marriage.

"I am happy for her. She definitely needs that," said Steve.

"Me, too. I wish her a happier life." Reggie, however, doubted if that would at all change her behavior in the future, but, for now, gave her the benefit of a doubt.

"Kim looks happy already, but she walked past us this morning without saying hi. Does that make sense?" asked Tina.

"Yes, it does," said Reggie. "You don't belong to her world yet."

That sent Tina a negative expression of Kim. "Purr! What world does she belong in? I better quit." Tina disgraced Kim for her unfriendly behavior.

"I learned she got engaged to a congressman named Devon. Do you know him?" asked Reggie.

"Everybody in this town knows Devon," said Steve.

"But I don't, sincerely speaking," answered Tina.

"It's only because you don't belong to the nightclubs."

"I'm glad. You better not," said Steve.

"I heard of him, but never saw him in person. Some ladies said he trashed one of his fiancées like an empty beer can shortly after their engagement," added Reggie.

"Wow! That was disgracing and preposterous. What kind of a representative is he?" asked Tina.

"He represents district seven. They call him Honorable Congressman Devon Killinga."

Steve laughed, and so did Reggie and Tina. Their fun soon changed to doubts over what would happen to Kim if this same congressman had dumped a previous fiancée. They also knew that Kim wasn't an easy person to let Devon get away without bruises should he try that on her.

Miki also told Kim that Devon had an affair with the mistress of the deceased front-runner, who would have probably represented district seven if he had lived. Devon, however, had no hand in that murder, although it paved the way to Washington.

Unfortunately for Steve, Reggie, and Tina, Kim's engagement to Devon soon turned out to be an empowerment for her to step up her intimidation and aggression at workplace and residential areas as well. Kim instructed her landlord not to allow other residents to park at her spot so Devon wouldn't need to look for a parking spot. That was granted. She requested for some of her neighbors to be moved to other apartments because they were noisy. That was also carried out promptly.

Devon bought her a new Lincoln SUV for the engagement gift. The SUV always sat in the parking lot with no other cars around. She quickly dominated the decision-making apparatus of the apartment complex. She even attempted to change the name of the driveway to the apartment from Babylon Drive to Killinga Drive. Cars moved to the far right whenever she pulled in, and pedestrians stopped to see her pass by.

Kim talked with authority at workplace. She once made a statement that she would change some of the laws that governed the foster care and adoption procedures in the state. Many workers were already upset by her excessive activities in the executive branch of the department. She asked the assistant commissioner to create a senior position within the department for her or else she would have it done from the top level of the government. She meant the governor, a friend to Devon.

"Just go ahead and create the position," said Kim.

"We don't create positions here, young lady," replied the assistant commissioner.

"Call me Ms. Killinga, sir," she replied angrily.

"You mean Congressman Killinga?" the assistant commissioner asked.

"Now you are talking," she replied with an intimidating smile enough to send a clear message to the assistant commissioner that she meant business.

"Okay, Madame Killinga, what we can do is only to propose and leave creation of the position to the human resources department," said the assistant commissioner.

"Do the proposal, and leave the rest to me."

Kim left the assistant commissioner's office and went back to her office that had now become too small for her. Two hours later, Kim went back to the assistant commissioner's office.

"Excuse me, Mr. Assistant Commissioner." She looked straight into the eyes of this already nervous man.

"Yes, Madame, what else can I do for you?" The assistant commissioner rose with both hands on top of his desk.

"Just a simple question, sir," she responded with a kind of authority even the commissioner of DCS wouldn't show to the subordinate.

"Okay, if I have the answer for you." The assistant commissioner let Kim spell out what she again was there for.

"How long have you been with the department?" Kim asked.

"Ten long years."

"Sounds like not too long though, does it?"

The assistant commissioner was quiet.

"Sorry. I meant in government service."

"Yes, ten years, as I said earlier." He felt like Kim was intimidating him. "I'm sorry. I have to leave for another meeting right now."

He got up from his chair and expected Kim to do the same. But he was wrong. Kim never moved an inch.

She instead asked another question. "We have people who have worked in this department for their entire life, but never got that far. Imagine retiring as case manager two after working hard for forty years. Is that rational?"

"What has that got to do with me, Madame?" The assistant commissioner looked a little irritated by her constant intrusion.

"To do with you or not, I will come back for the answer. You better be ready for it." She left immediately.

The assistant commissioner was relieved. He grabbed his documents and rushed for the meeting next door.

Kim soon found herself as defender of the voiceless old guards of the DCS. They secretly pumped her to voice what they themselves couldn't openly say or present to the leadership. She took whatever they wanted to say and presented it with vigor. Her target point was the assistant commissioner, who was young and had not been in the government service long enough to defend his rise to the very position he held. It was an executive position, but he was pole-vaulted from among the pool of directors who had been with the department for three or four decades.

Kim was particularly upset when she learned a lady who was hired after her got a position of program manager, a position that was never advertised for other qualified candidates to apply and compete for.

"How could they possibly do that?" she asked.

"DCS doesn't need what you call a formal procedure," one of the associates said.

"Formal or not, we need transparency. Employees have the right to know of any position that needs to be filled in this department." Kim had already forgotten how she was promoted to the supervisor position.

"Leave that for the owners." The associate then left.

The associate wouldn't poke her nose into issues beyond her reach. But, for Kim, it was just the beginning. She wanted promotion, and she had to make her feelings known in the months to come.

Steve, Reggie, and Tina were no longer her immediate targets. As a matter of fact, she no longer ran after them as she looked for the bigger personalities to wrestle with. But she was still the unit supervisor. She didn't call the meetings regularly, but flooded her staff with e-mail messages and phone calls. Steve liked the idea of e-mails, but not the phone calls.

"I hate being called just to find out whether I'm in the office or not," said Steve.

"Just say present and hang up the phone." Tina also received that kind of call from Kim a couple times.

"Is that how you respond every time she called?"

"I'm here. That was my response to her."

Steve thought it was rude and unprofessional to respond that way on the public phone that were often taped or listened to by monitors. "Don't do that, Tina. These phones are being recorded for quality purposes."

Clients often got employees fired because of inappropriate phone conversations. Messing with Kim on phone would easily land them into real trouble.

"Just respond to whatever she wants you to do. After all, she's no longer arrogant the way she used to be," said Reggie.

Reggie seemed to have spoken too early. The next morning, Kim summoned all three to her office and blasted them for poor performances and unauthorized use of office phones for private calls.

"I told you. This woman will never change," said Tina.

"No one said that. We thought she was gradually moving away from her past, which, of course, wasn't the case, as we found out this morning," said Reggie.

"Keep up the good work, girls. I know we will beat this weather one day." Steve assured Reggie and Tina of his faith in them.

They had become like young sisters to him. They always sought his advice and support. Steve sat with the two girls and started narrating some qualities a supervisor needed to possess. "Not knowing your boundaries of responsibility and power limitation are some of the worse practices that supervisors pursue. To consider oneself a supervisor is one thing; to be looked upon by others as a supervisor is another thing else. Kim could consider herself a supervisor by literally occupying that position. It's better to call her a coincidental supervisor. The best supervisory practices begin with self-organization and self-respect, the dignity that comes from inside you. In order to be a good supervisor, Kim needs to have a clear understanding of how to exert positive impact upon the employees who will, in return, accept her as their team leader and not as the boss as such." Steve paused.

"A flow of mutual understanding and respect between her and us could often produce good results and promote cooperation among members of this unit, but, unfortunately, Kim never took that opportunity to inspire her group that I feel would have possibly changed the group dynamics. She worked repeatedly toward building the stumbling blocks between herself and the group members. Her one year as head of the unit would have served her well, especially in the areas of learning from our group and building trust across the aisle." He stopped because their break time was running out. Everyone went back to the office.

One morning, Kim picked a baseless confrontation with an office cleaner that quickly turned ugly. The housekeeper was doing her routine work when Kim arrogantly shouted at the housekeeper, as she often did.

"Hey, you janitor!" she called aloud.

The cleaner didn't hear because she was vacuuming in one of the offices.

"Hey, you Mexican janitor, I'm talking to you. Are you deaf?" She approached the housekeeper, grabbed her by the shoulder, and twisted her around violently.

The housekeeper stopped the vacuum cleaner. "Ma'am, my name is Lorena, not Mexican janitor."

"I wanted to draw your attention after neglecting my calls for several times. Besides, I'm not interested in your Mexican name."

"Okay. Now I'm listening. What can I do for you?"

Kim remained silent and looked at the housekeeper in a demeaning way for some minutes before she started yelling. "Look at you. You're just a filthy piece of dirt trying to ignore me." She turned around and started going the opposite direction away from the scene. She turned toward Lorena. "I don't wanna waste my energy talking to you, janitor."

Lorena moved closer to her. "You called me, didn't you?"

"I did. And so what? I did call simply to let you know that my trashcan wasn't emptied for the last three days, and I wanna see it emptied right away. Do you understand what I just said?"

Kim had never learned the art of communicating with workers from outside her workplace. She scorned at everyone who came her way, let alone her target group that had already become immune to whatever she did.

"No, ma'am. Could you please repeat it once again?"

Kim went nuts. She took two deep breaths and then burst into rage. "Get out of my sight, cockroach."

Kim was enraged. Her face looked like a fleeing convict who had just broken out of the jail and was ready to take down anybody standing in her way. Her insults agitated the housekeeper. She, however, remained composite. She moved slowly as she pushed her cart toward Kim's cubicle. She wanted to do some cleaning in some of the nearby offices, including Kim's. Without any warning, Kim got a three-hole metal puncher and flung it at the housekeeper. It landed on her right shoulder. That was enough to set fire in the house. In no time, Lorena grabbed the wet mop from the bucket underneath her cart and hit Kim in the face repeatedly until Kim ran for a cover behind the refrigerator, but Lorena followed with the mop, still handy for the second round of the fiasco.

"This is what I do for mean office ladies like you. I brush them clean like a toilet tub." She pinned Kim against the refrigerator with a plunger as she continued to squeeze the wet mop against her face.

Reggie heard the scuffle and ran to stop the fight. She pulled Lorena off from Kim, whose face was wet. The water from the soaked mop dripped into Kim's wide-open, push-up bra, and she looked just like something out of a septic tank. Kim wiped her face and immediately realized that Reggie was there, still restraining Lorena from attacking her any further.

Like a wildcat, Kim jumped from her position and tried to attack the housekeeper, but she missed. The blow landed on Reggie's face and sent her down on her knees.

"Why are you doing this to me?" Reggie asked.

"Because you sided with her in the fight against me," said Kim with a kind of vengeance.

"She never took a side in this fight. Besides, you don't need two people to beat the hell out of you," said Lorena.

She threatened Kim with the mop. Kim dived under the breakfast table. She got up from there and then tried to attack the housekeeper once again. She missed the target. She ended up on the cart for a short, wild ride, scattering the cleaning stuff on it as she struggled to stop the runaway cart. It finally stopped by the side of a multipurpose copier machine. Kim quickly got off the cart and escaped into her cubicle, terrified. The housekeeper knew the fight was virtually over. She went and got her cart. She stacked all the scattered stuff back onto the cart and pushed it away. Kim stared as the housekeeper slowly disappeared between the cubicles beyond.

A fight at the workplace is degrading, especially when it involves an office worker and a vendor. Moments after the incident, Lorena filed a complaint against Kim with her office. Kim never reported it to the director, as stipulated in the DCS policy. It wasn't immediately clear if Kim ignored the reporting procedure or if she were ignorant of the procedural steps to be taken. Reggie simply put it as a guilty conscious that resulted from her unprecedented behavior toward Lorena. Friends urged Kim to apologize to Lorena and avoid the pending legal actions in the court and the office's disciplinary action. She reluctantly accepted. One of her friends called for a conciliatory meeting between Kim and Lorena, and Reggie was called as a witness. Kim apologized, and Lorena accepted the apology and then dropped the case.

Reggie, Tina, and Steve got together for lunch the following morning at a nearby restaurant when Reggie started telling her story to the other two. "Have you heard about the fight between Kim and Lorena last Monday?" Reggie paused. "We were in a conciliatory meeting yesterday morning."

"I only heard there was some disagreement between her and Lorena and nothing else," said Tina.

"I did hear about that, but I wasn't sure it involved a fistfight," added Steve.

"Yes. It was a real fight, and I was kinda caught up in the cross fire," Reggie said.

"You mean that prominent bump on your forehead?" asked Tina.

Reggie knocked her head twice in an answer.

"What did you do in return?" Tina asked her in an inciting manner.

"Who gave that good stamp on you, Reggie?" asked Steve.

"Kim did." Reggie answered. She knew Tina would criticize her for not paying back. "I tried to restrain Lorena from assaulting her further. She was already acting defensive when, all of sudden, she sprang on her feet and tried to hit Lorena. She missed Lorena, and the shot, unfortunately, ended up on my face. It was like a horse kick that sent me down, like a losing gladiator." She stopped for a few seconds. "She never apologized, but accused me instead of siding with Lorena against her. I was so mad at her, but I controlled my anger."

"I'm sorry to hear that, but you did the right thing. Kim would never apologize to you openly, but would rather take the guilty conscious," said Steve.

Tina was clinching her fingers. For her, Reggie could have at least given Kim a good left hook on that tainted chin or at least a right kick in the butt. Tina even wondered what had become of Reggie, her friend whose anger was always at the fingertips.

"Why did you attend that conciliatory meeting when she accused you of siding with Lorena against her?" Tina wanted Reggie to distance herself from Kim altogether.

"I just wanted to be part of the team that promotes peaceful coexistence at the workplace. Besides, Kim is still one of us, and we wouldn't like to see her locked behind bars."

"That explains everything, Reggie. People learn from good examples and not the bad ones. What you did probably sent her a message of how you still care for her despite all the evils she committed against you. I'm proud of the good example you have shown. I, for one, would do the same," Steve lamented.

"Playing good guys, eh? It's still too soon to give a pat on the back. She's not done with you yet, Reggie. It's just a matter of time, and she'll strike again." Tina was never satisfied for letting Kim get away with that.

They talked for the entire lunch break until it was about time to report to work. They encouraged Reggie to be vigilant and keep her distance from Kim. They got to the office close to one o'clock. Kim was already there with the logbook in hand, doing her usual roll calls. She ogled as they passed by. She immediately put the log back on the counter for them to sign in after their lunch. She wouldn't say anything as the three came back in time, in fact, still with five minutes left from their lunch break. But she still managed to squeeze her aggressive approach through.

In a brief e-mail she sent to Steve, Reggie, and Tina, she stated, "I'm very disappointed to learn that y'all still neglect my office orders. I have made it clear that you three shouldn't go for lunch at the same time. We need someone to cover the office while the other two are out for lunch. Let this message serve as a second warning to all of you."

She sent the message first with a copy to the director, but immediately retrieved it from all the recipients' mailboxes. She deleted the director's address and resent the mail to the three members only.

Steve was the first to realize that a message had popped up. Before he could open, it was gone and only popped up again after few minutes. He also realized the director was not served with a copy. Steve knew office procedures better than Kim did. As usual, he didn't take it seriously. He also asked the other two to be calm and never to respond to the message. They proved right. Kim was just trying to create fear by some of her messages, which were nothing but mere threats. That was why she removed the name of the director from the recipient list.

Devon was back in town, and Kim took off three days in a row to spend quality time with him. That was like a summer break for Steve, Reggie, and Tina. They spent their short breaks together and went out for lunch without being harassed upon their return to the office. Everything went smoothly. Even Amy and Vicky had noticed the difference of how happy and peaceful the unit was with the absence of Kim. Steve was a very knowledgeable lead worker with the experience that would easily earn him a supervisory position in the department.

Vicky and Amy arranged to go out together one Saturday evening. They chose to shop at their neighborhood mall in the evening. They shopped for an hour and then decided to go back to Amy's apartment to spend the rest of their evening. After talking about a range of topics, Amy came up with something that had bothered her for quite some time.

"Vicky, why do things look completely different with Kim's absence?"

"Because everybody hates Kim." Vicky paused for a little. "Kim seems to have made more enemies than friends in this short period as the supervisor of the unit."

"That could also mean we are her only friends, aren't we?"

"I don't think so. I'm not a friend as such, but something in between, an associate if you will." Vicky paused.

"Aha! Is that your new terminology for loyalty or what?"

"For your information please, I never pledged any allegiance of loyalty to her. I would never ever do such a thing in my entire life."

"Wow! I can't believe you could turn your back to Kim that fast." Amy was confused about her position as Vicky was gradually pulling away from the coalition. She, however, remained undecided as she tried to assert her position. "It isn't fair to desert a friend in the face of trouble, am I right?"

"No, you aren't. I already told you that I'm not her friend at all. Besides, I have given her more than I got in return." Vicky was upset, especially with Kim's senseless fight with Lorena. For her, Kim was a troublemaker, and she wouldn't like to identify with her as such.

"That's quite ridiculous. What has gone wrong with you?" asked Amy.

"Do you see anything wrong in my judgments lately? Just tell me."

Vicky wasn't backing down anytime soon. Whatever effort Amy tried to make wouldn't persuade her, but it would be a waste of time. Amy stopped any further embarrassment by not pressing on that topic any further. Kim was obviously losing her base from within, and Amy herself was hanging loose without the backing from her closest friend.

After exhausting that sensitive topic, Amy and Vicky went into the kitchen to prepare some dinner. They got some food and went back to the living room to eat while watching the bikini contest on television. Both seemed to like the program.

"Wow! That one looks cute. I kinda like her boobs." Amy held her shrunken ones in her palms.

"Sorry, not those ones, but look at these."

Vicky grabbed both of her boobs, jacked them upwards, and then shook them violently inside her loose bra. It was an amazing and awesome demonstration of talent mania. Amy immediately conceded as though they were in a real contest. Vicky would have even shown her underwear if Amy were to insist. They continued to watch the program until it was over. Then Amy's cell phone rang. She checked the caller ID. It was Kim calling from her cell phone.

"Hello, sunshine," Kim said.

"Hi, Ms. Kim, how are you doing?" asked Amy.

"I'm doing wonderful. As you know, just relaxing with my babe," she proudly exclaimed. Amy heard her say to Devon, "She is my closest friend in the whole department." Then she got back with Amy. "What are your plans for tonight? My fiancé and I are going out for dinner.

Would you like to join us? If you do, he has a friend who would be interested in you. Check it out, girl." She laughed. That made Amy even more annoyed, but she never hung up on her.

"No, thank you, Kim. My boyfriend is back from Iraq, and he's coming over. We are going out for a date."

"Oh really? Do you now have a boyfriend? I thought you still hung around with Vicky, that friend of yours."

She paused to get a kiss from Devon. She soon forgot that Amy was with her on phone. She let the phone slip on the bed and never hung up.

Amy heard Kim say to Devon, "You just tell your friend to go ahead and arrange a big surprise for her. I mean, something like a car that would easily blow her away."

"I don't think that's a good idea. Besides, my friend is happily married, and I sincerely respect that," Devon reacted sharply.

Kim backed off, but only for that time though.

"That was a mere favor for him, just for one night. He will carry on with his life."

Amy hung up. She didn't like to hear Kim setting her up anymore. She felt like she was being betrayed, and she immediately believed that Vicky was absolutely right for refusing to be closer to Kim. That was enough reason for her to sever her relationship with Kim as well. Vicky realized the troubles in Amy's eyes, but never interfered. She knew Amy had talked to Kim on the phone, and something probably made her upset. Amy rose from her seat and went to the bathroom. She flushed cold water on her face, wiped it dry, and came back to the living room.

"I am sorry. I was a little upset," she said.

"I saw that in your eyes. What went wrong in your conversation with Kim?"

"She tried to sell me into prostitution or trade me for sex in exchange for favor."

"You mean like setting you up with another man for sex?"

"Exactly right. She was trying to hook me up for sex with Devon's friend, a rich, fat rat named Big Daddy. Devon disliked her idea though."

"Oh my goodness! How's that gonna work? Don't tell me anymore. Kim is such a devil."

Vicky was relieved that Amy had come to know Kim's true colors. She also warned Amy to play it cool, like she didn't overhear the conversation with Devon. It was approaching midnight, and Vicky excused herself to go home. She promised to check on Amy again after Sunday prayers. Amy walked her to the door and let her go to the car right at the front of her apartment. She locked the door and went straight to bed for the night.

Devon left for Washington that Sunday evening. Kim was on her own once again. She had lost Katie for good, and her other associates were on the verge of deserting her as well. Vicky for sure had made up her mind earlier never to maintain close acquaintances with Kim anymore. Amy was convinced beyond a doubt that hanging with Kim could be dangerous and unpleasant. She, however, needed to adopt an exit strategy that wouldn't leave her vulnerable to retaliatory actions by Kim.

Kim called Amy's cell phone twice that Sunday night, but Amy never picked up the calls. Kim's unwarranted plans and the despicable comments still enraged her. Kim left a message on Amy's voice mail in her last call, expressing how she missed her and how she had expected her to show up so they could hang out together.

"Show your face out there, girl. You never know. Luck might be waiting for you, sweetie."

It was then clear to Amy that Kim was working hard to sell her to Big Daddy even against Devon's objection. She began digesting the motive behind Kim's plan, and she soon came across one, something Kim had talked about one day. Kim had been promised something big whenever she closed a deal on her. A one-night deal was enough in order for her to get a new Mercedes-Benz she had yearned for quite some time.

Amy saved the message, but never called Kim back. She instead shared the message with Vicky, who once again advised her not to react right out, but to let Kim start feeling that something was terribly wrong with her perception of Amy. She agreed and promised not to approach Kim over her ill-intended plans. Kim, on the other side, was crossing her fingers and praying hard to have Amy take the deal, as her dreams for a Mercedes-Benz squarely lay on her. She even planned to use her position, if necessary, to get Amy into accepting the man.

"After all, it would only be a matter of just a one- or two-hour ride with that kind of big bone," Kim thought to herself.

Big Daddy was Devon's benefactor and close friend. He had been the financial backbone for Devon ever since Devon planned to run for the public office. His coming to town could probably be for a refill, as he was running low on funds. Devon told Kim about his friend and how indispensable Big Daddy was for his success in the last elections. Kim also wanted to get her share of the loot without Devon's involvement by giving away Amy as a small favor.

Monday wasn't a pleasant day for Amy. She was down and avoided any form of contacts with Kim, who tried to get to her by all means. She sent an e-mail to Kim saying she wasn't feeling well and would like to go and see her doctor right away. Kim approved her request. She hurriedly left for home before Kim could get to her office. Kim called Amy's cell phone when she failed to catch up with her, but she never picked up the call. She even blocked her voice mail so Kim could not leave any message on the machine. Kim went to ask Vicky about the nature of Amy's illness, but Vicky pretended not to have heard from Amy since morning. Kim felt sorry for Amy and then retreated to her office. She felt uneasy because she promised Big Daddy that Amy would be ready in her house for delivery that Monday evening. Now Amy wouldn't be there as she planned. What would come next? A little offer from her own reserved jar could perhaps do the trick if both of them would keep their mouths shut for the rest of their lives.

Kim went home that Monday evening, took a bath, and lit some candles for a romantic night. She wore cologne that could drive Big Daddy sky-high. She sat there ready and waiting to make the ultimate sacrifice for the night. Big Daddy showed up at around midnight and immediately realized that Kim was all by herself and in pink lingerie. She walked up to him and led him to the couch. Then she let him touch her naked thighs. She rose and went to the table across the living room and brought him a glass of fine wine. Then she held him by the arm, and both disappeared into the bedroom. She took off his shoes, his necktie, shirt, and pants.

Big Daddy finally stopped her momentarily. "What are you doing, ma'am?"

"What do you think am I doing? Just trying to make your night easy, Big Daddy."

"I appreciate all the kindness you have shown me, but we don't need to go this far. You know it would be difficult to stop a runaway train once it takes off."

He cautioned her repeatedly, but Kim was defiantly determined never to let the keys for a Mercedes-Benz slip through her fingers. She had the beauty and the language that went with it.

"Just a flavor of it, and we will quit forever," she insisted.

By then, she had managed to strip him naked. Big Daddy gave in, and the rest was history. He felt guilty for going behind the back of his longtime friend and ending up in bed with his fiancée. He remained in bed thinking hard and then quickly brushed everything from his mind.

He said to himself, "This is the game of the City Boyz. Besides, Devon himself does that to his other friends all the time."

He turned around and got Kim again. Now she knew the big fish was securely zipped in her net for good. For Kim, it was all about fun and the excitement she had with Big Daddy. That also marked the beginning of the long journey they would have together in the future. Kim came to like Big Daddy even more than her fiancé mainly because he was closer to her and had all the attention she wanted. He kept sneaking behind Devon whenever he was away in Washington.

Big Daddy once remarked, "Make the laws in Washington, and I will execute them here at home for you."

This meant Devon could care for his job in Washington while Big Daddy took care of Kim at home. Kim had gotten her dream Mercedes-Benz and didn't care how she acquired it. After all, she had a congressman for a fiancé behind her back.

Kim had already established herself with some royalties from Big Daddy, who also had his share of Kim whenever Devon was away. In fact, Big Daddy was getting even the lion share of Devon's woman. Big Daddy had a house on the outskirts of the town where he and Kim escaped for some weekends. He told his wife he was traveling for business trips, but ended up within the city limits. Kim had already become obsessed with him. Despite her new lifestyle, Kim maintained her attendance and punctuality at record high. She was so elusive that nobody could detect her underground activities, especially with Vicky and Amy now virtually gone.

Big Daddy was a man of his words. He didn't even pay attention to Kim in public. He never called her on his cell phone. Instead, he made calls from public phone booths or just borrowed one from someone. He also asked Kim to do the same when calling him. That virtually made it impossible for his wife or Devon to suspect their affair. Kim's secret relationship with Big Daddy continued to flourish over the crumbling relationship with Devon who was, by large, a carefree man when it came to some dubious relationships with women. He for sure would rather lose Kim to Big Daddy than lose him as a friend.

The two managed their secret love well, and Kim kept evading Devon, who also had another woman in his life in Washington that Kim didn't know about. But Big Daddy knew the secret of Devon in and out. The other woman sometimes came to the town for two or three days of vacation under the care of Big Daddy, who made hotel reservations in advance without Kim's knowledge. He even came to like the game more because, whenever Devon came to town unannounced, he confined himself in a hotel in an isolated part of the city. Big Daddy would have Kim all for himself.

But Devon didn't want Kim to get pregnant then, but Big Daddy did because his wife hadn't given him a child since their marriage five years ago. Kim was also in no hurry for a baby because she wanted to be walked down the aisle in a church wedding.

Chapter Five

Manpower Reduction Task Force

The economic downturn had caused many companies to downsize or go out of business altogether. Many family members lost their jobs and turned to public assistance for their living. The state government was also bracing with loss in parts of their federal funding. A 4 percent reduction in workforce was eminent. The DCS commissioner issued a memorandum for individual departments to identify some possible areas that needed to be trimmed in the face of the oncoming reduction due in six months. The departmental directors requested all unit managers and supervisors to assist in the preliminary planning process to be presented to the senior management discussions. A task force was formed. Kim represented her unit.

Kim unilaterally established herself as the leader of the task force. She sent an e-mail to all the members to attend an important meeting for debriefing and group assignments. The director appreciated her prompt action, but her self-appointment as the team leader was viewed with skepticism though. Kim asked the director to chair the meeting and with her as the moderator. Their first meeting went well. They laid down ground rules and strategies to identify which of the areas and positions that needed to be trimmed. Kim immediately sprang up without requesting permission to speak from the chairperson.

"I will sacrifice three positions from my own unit, actually four. Details will be provided to support my proposal."

"Excuse me, Kim. What are you talking about?" the director asked.

Kim tried to remember where that idea came from. "It was actually the 4 percent reduction of the manpower required of each unit to come up with."

"That looks like 80 percent of the labor force in your unit," said one of the members.

"Yes, assuming Kim was long gone before effecting the 80 percent reduction in her unit," a second member responded cunningly.

"Sincerely speaking, we can also amalgamate several units to give us a smaller structure of the department, which will also imply fewer supervisors on the ground," the director commented to give the task force a heads-up of what other areas were to look for.

'Oh, man, did you just say we have to fire ourselves even before completing this task?" said one of the male representatives.

He thought that, whenever a department planned for downsizing, it was always the grassroots that had to be laid off. But who was Kim going to supervise if 80 percent of her subordinates were laid off? The remaining one person could be attached with another unit, and Kim had to disappear in thin air.

"Important units like mine are the backbone of this department. The director knows that very well. Tempering with these vital units will destabilize the department, not to mention the children currently being served. As we deliberate in this session, I warn you to exercise extra caution to tempering with these units of vital importance." Kim looked confident after delivering that speech.

She tried everything to have Steve, Reggie, and Tina laid off, along with her emerging enemy, Vicky, whom she accused of inciting Amy against her. She planned to keep Amy around for some personal gains, but not as Big Daddy's mistress this time. Kim had even thought of what mess she would have caused if she were to relinquish Big Daddy to Amy. For sure, she would have probably ordered herself shot execution style. She couldn't afford seeing another lady with Big Daddy without cursing, not even his own wife, whom Kim now referred to as the "barren barrel," or simply *ba-ba*.

Big Daddy cautioned her many times not to use that derogatory name about his wife, but Kim preferred using the name to literally have Big Daddy turn his back against his wife. Someone like Big Daddy who had successfully managed his wealth to the extent of becoming rich could no doubt manage his own affairs well. The pressure from a woman like Kim wouldn't have any serious impact on him at all. He knew very well that someone who had sold herself at the cost of a Mercedes-Benz could no doubt sleep with another man who offered her a train engine or a Cessna plane. He compared Kim to his wife and looked at the differences between the two. Then he quickly concluded that having his wife in life, even without children, was more pleasant than having Kim with ten children and a 100 percent chance of him ending up dead in the hands of the contract assassins just because Kim would like to have the wealth all for herself.

In their second session, the senior management came up with a resolution that all the permanent employees of the department should be given the chance for voluntary termination of services with the exchange for some rewards, a package known as buyout. They unanimously targeted vacant positions on the nominal rolls and interim positions for the layoffs. The resolution was communicated to the middle management for implementation at the lower level of the management where Kim was a self-appointed leader of her group. She called for a meeting to disseminate the resolution from the senior management to her group members.

"Thank y'all for showing up at this meeting." She looked around and noticed that some members haven't arrived yet. "I wouldn't rather wear a watch if I couldn't keep my own time."

The group laughed.

One of them asked, "What time are we supposed to be here?"

Kim looked at her time. "Two o'clock to be exact. It's now five minutes after two."

She was damn wrong. Kim had set her watch five minutes ahead of the time to confront Steve and the two girls for late arrival, but forgot to reset it when they came back from lunch fifteen minutes early.

"Kim, you really don't need to wear that watch. Do you?" asked a member.

"This is an Omega wristwatch, the kind that scientists recommend for the astronauts to wear. It's not the ordinary watches that state employees wear." She paused for while. "I'm sorry to say this, but this is how it is." She extended her left arm to one of the members sitting next to her. "Be my witness, Nancy. Have I pronounced your name correctly?"

Before Natalie could respond to the question, Kim reached over to her state-issued ID badge dangling on a short lace around the neck and pulled it toward her. "Hmm, I guess I have pronounced your name wrong."

Natalie retrieved her badge from Kim's hand.

"The Omega watch spins out of control, and the state employees go by the real time. Have you seen how amazing it is?" one of the ladies said.

Kim immediately realized she had not reset her time back, so she did. All of sudden, she saw the other three members enter the conference room. She had nothing left to complain about.

She opened the meeting and announced what was required of the lower management. "Folks, the senior management has delegated me to make sure that no permanent state employees should be laid off whatsoever the case. I'm glad they took that piece of advice I gave them prior to their deliberations this morning."

Kim was an opportunist. She had never met with any member of the senior management team that very morning. She wanted to take credit for everything.

"Excuse me, ma'am, did you just say you have met with one or a group of the senior management this morning?" one member asked.

Very excitedly, Kim responded, "I gladly did that on behalf of the task force, and they appreciated what I offered them. That was why they came up with that resolution." She felt confident.

"What does our bylaw section 4A, reading together with section 7C, say about the disclosure of any information in part or as a whole in the activities of the task force?" a member asked.

Kim had no idea what the member was talking about. She took the bylaws and the procedural notes home, but never read them. She sat there and waited to have someone help in answering that question.

"Any decision made by the task force should be disclosed in a joint communiqué with the senior management. Any disclosure by an individual member in the absence of its members is a violation and, therefore, null and void," Natalie spelled out by heart.

That stunned everybody. Natalie was a former nun with Sacred Heart Sisters, and she had memorized the entire Bible by heart. So the twenty-page bylaws were just a piece of cake for her. She still wore long dresses and headdress the old-fashioned way. Her boyfriend advised her to wear pointed shoes to line up her chicken feet toes.

"Wow! That was impressive. I never knew we would come to the point of revisiting these bylaws one day," Kim commented.

"From the account we have just heard, it seems like some parts of the bylaws have been violated," a male member of the task force asked.

"In part or as a whole, I may say yes," Natalie responded.

She wanted Kim to explain why she did release the information against the regulations. Kim was finally forced to defend her. The group underestimated Kim from the very beginning for not being smart. Kim was smarter than most, if not all, of them. First, she managed to impose herself on them as the leader. Second, they never questioned her legitimacy for being their leader. Finally, their silence legitimized Kim's proclamation as the leader of the team and the absolute voice of the group. The members were no match to Kim, the lady who had positioned herself to manage love affairs with two powerful men. She had dismissed all the members, but she considered Natalie as a pain in ass. She knew she had to get her by the tail this time. She started by going after Natalie's personality to discredit her and shut her up for good.

"Natalie should first tell us why she failed to follow the rules of the church when she became pregnant and was expelled disgracefully from the nunnery. Cramming of the Bible by heart without understanding is like a Xerox copier machine that doesn't distinguish between the pages. She slept with a priest and got pregnant just because the priest told her that God sent him to redeem her from the sins of the world. She never even questioned or used her common sense, which I believe she doesn't have. What I did was a time-saving action. You better call it rapid reaction. I did it for all of us. When I shine, you shine. Remember your own slogan of, 'One for all and all for one.' Did I come up with that slogan? No. It wasn't me, but it was the idea of Natalie who also coined those words. I never gave the whole story to the senior management, but only a hint. Y'all know how good I am in generating valuable information. My fiancé, Big Daddy, even depends on me when comes to good advice." She made a gaffe and immediately retracted her statement. "Oops, I meant my fiancé, Congressman Devon. Not his friend, Big Daddy."

That, however, had already hurt her credibility because Devon and Big Daddy were two different sides of the same coin.

Natalie broke down in tears at Kim's character assassination that left her areas of weakness open. She had tried over many years to come to terms with her past and open a new chapter in her life, but now that seemed not to be working either. Wherever she went, the community looked upon her as a sinner of the highest order, even worse than those who killed Jesus. She tried to disguise herself from head to toe by covering her whole body, but that only traversed her into criticisms by her female friends and only boyfriend as well, who nicknamed her a "ninja woman warrior." Natalie never saw the priest once they were expelled from the church.

Kim never stopped there. "Natalie, can you tell us what happened to the baby?"

Natalie and the priest had dumped the baby into the latrine pit immediately after the child was born and left the child there to die.

Fortunately, one of the nuns heard a baby crying deep in the latrine beneath and reported the news to the Mother Superior. The child was later rescued. Natalie and the priest were expelled from the church and deported from Papua New Guinea back to the United State. The child was placed in a undisclosed location for the sake of the church and the safety of the child as well. Natalie continued to live in self-denial with no child, no husband, and no dreams of her aspirations.

"We don't need all those explanation in the private life of our group members. All what is needed right here right now is whether a member of the committee broke a law or not," one member flared at Kim.

"I love people who don't use their common sense because no one would blame them for all the stupid comments that have come to dominate our discussions. Having said that, I would sincerely appreciate if one could just keep the damn, rotten mouth shut from revealing those colorful teeth that unleash some awful odors." Kim lashed out on the last speaker for her lack of knowledge and belonging to the rank-and-file members of the colonial leftovers.

That was a violation of the article that forbids discrimination of the state employees against race, religion, sex, ethnicity, age, and many more. The elderly lady rose from her seat and adjusted her bifocal glasses twice to get a good look at Kim.

"Young lady, I have seen the day, and I'm proud to have said that. The love of the people lies in your own mouth, whether you like it or not. You have made a mockery of yourself by looking down upon others just to cover your ignorance and inability to manage your own affairs. I am now requesting a vote of no confidence. I just need to see a capable member from within this group to take over the functions of the facilitator with immediate effect."

Another member immediately seconded the move. "I'm with you. I don't even see the need for a vote to remove her. We never elected her, and we should just select her replacement."

The group quickly moved forward to nominate Kim's replacement, and they unanimously chose Natalie for the office. Kim remained on her seat transfixed, not knowing what to say. With that embarrassment, she decided to quit the group and disgracefully left the conference room. The task force members never saw her in their meetings again. The director also gave her a verbal warning about her misconduct and deserting the task force without prior notice to the director. Kim requested two days off, and it was approved.

She called Big Daddy and wanted him to arrange for some sort of getaway to another state for three days. He was handy and booked the air tickets and hotel reservation for three nights in Las Vegas. Big Daddy told his wife that he was traveling for a business trip that would last for about a week. He added that he would let her know in case he cut the trip short. They left the following morning. His wife offered to drop off Big Daddy at the airport, but he declined the offer. He preferred a park-and-fly garage where he sometimes parked whenever he went on trips that lasted for a week or less.

Kim and Big Daddy spent three days in Las Vegas and came back on the fourth day. No questions were asked. Kim did the right thing. She called the director and requested two additional days off against her annual leave while in Nevada. She was rejuvenated when she reported to work after her brief vacation. Amy and Vicky wondered why Kim changed some of her approaches. She responded to questions from her staff and some of her friends in other units.

"Why does she look so different today?" asked Amy.

"Because your eyes were not accustomed to her in the last few days," answered Vicky.

"You may be right. A lioness is a lioness," responded Amy.

Both she and Amy walked away from the scene.

Chapter Six

The Fight for Position

A retiree, who had served the DCS for fifty years, almost double Kim's age, vacated a program manager position. Kim asked Judy some months before she announced her retirement if she planned to take her position with her to the grave.

"Why can't you retire and enjoy a peaceful retirement for the rest of your few remaining years?" asked Kim.

Surprised by that careless question coming from someone who claimed to be a supervisor, Judy stared at Kim quietly for two minutes. "I will hold on to this position until a good and competent person comes around."

That statement insulted Kim, but she hung around to engage her in further conversation. "I have a master's degree in psychology, and I have worked diligently to promote the cause of this department. I guess I deserve a reward for this, in monetary form or promotion, but I prefer the latter."

"Hmm, a master's degree is good for wall decoration. DCS needs practical experience with a good sense of humor," Judy said.

"The wallpaper is different, ma'am. What modern people present for employment are the transcripts. Let me ask you this. What kinda degree do you have?"

"I have a good fifty years of experience under my belt, and that overrides any kinds of all the forged and fictitious certificates the so called modern people present for employment in the so-called modern time."

Kim wanted Judy to look upon her as the ideal candidate for the position before she retired or even recommend her to the director for future promotion against that position. It wasn't only Judy that Kim had contacted. She was literally going after the elderly employees who were close to their retirement age, the same group she once advocated for not a long time ago. She probably had even wished some of them bad luck, literally death, so they could create some vacant positions.

"Death doesn't select. It doesn't discriminate between young and old either. It's like a time bomb that goes off when the clock ticks," one elderly lady told Kim when she tried to make jokes out of her decision to work in her late seventies.

Judy celebrated her diamond jubilee of service with her long-serving coworkers and all the friends and directors. Kim was also there expecting to hear if the magic word, "retirement," would come out of Judy's remarks. Fortunately, it did. Judy intended to retire one month after her fifty years of distinguished service with the department. She had given herself ample time for transition and handing over the office after fifty years of straight service. A week after her final departure from the department, the director sent a memo inviting applications from qualified and interested employees for the position. A promotional registry was opened for the position with the human resources Web site. Kim applied, but so did many other interested employees. Two weeks later, Kim received a regret letter stating she wasn't qualified for the position of the program manager at the time.

"What do they mean? If I don't, who does?" Kim related the content of the letter to Big Daddy.

"That's not the end of the world. Look at the bright side of you."

Big Daddy tried to console her and get her to understand that it was only one position against fifty or so applicants. Kim was so annoyed that she even wished Devon was around so she could use his status to maneuver her way into the register. She called the registry office and asked the lady who picked the phone. "What criteria did you use in assessing my credentials for the promotional position I applied for?"

The lady replied. "You still wouldn't qualify for the position even after five years because your certificate isn't from an accredited institution. Just forget referring to it as a master's degree.

Kim yelled, "If not master, what then? Cigar wrap? Fool."

Kim hung up on her and sat on the top of her desk with her legs wide open. She breathed rapidly like a desert lizard encountering a hundred and seventy-degree heat.

"How did they make that up? Bunch of idiots," she began talking to herself.

Her stressed miniskirt was already drawn to a dangerous position, but Kim never cared. She'd had a bad day already, and pulling the skirt back wouldn't make any difference. She sat there for quite some time uninterrupted until her office phone rang. She neglected the ring and never picked it up, but the phone continued ringing for quite some time. She reluctantly picked it up when she heard Big Daddy's voice leaving a message on her machine.

"Hey, baby." Kim immediately straightened up for a better conversation with Big Daddy.

"Hello, sweetie." Big Daddy put away the cup of tea he was sipping.

"What are you up to? Do you miss me? I know you do, and I miss you, too." She never gave him chance to respond until she was done.

"I'm just checking to see if you could meet me for dinner tonight. We haven't gotten together for so long."

"Where at?" She looked delighted, and she would have probably left the office if Big Daddy were to command her to do so.

"The usual place. Our usual getaway place around the—"

"Stop right there. I know what you are trying to tell me. I need something more than that for the night."

"You got it, baby. Hilton Resort Suites. How about that?"

"Yes! That's perfect, babe."

"Okay, let's meet there at seven o'clock tonight." He hung up the phone.

Kim held the handset in her hand for some time before placing it back on the base. That call was a lifesaver. It took off the load that was crushing her, and now she had to concentrate on her date with her emerging star, the number two man in her life and someone who was about to literally snatch her away from her would-be husband.

Kim met Big Daddy that evening. They had a good dinner and spent the night together at the hotel. Fridays were good weekdays, and Kim had nothing to worry about Saturday. The two-night deal wasn't over yet. They had breakfast together that Saturday morning before Big Daddy could leave for a series of his business appointments. He left Kim behind, still compensating the hours from the previous night. She woke up late. After taking a shower, she left for home.

A week later, Kim received an apology letter in the mail from human resources, stating the first letter was generated in error and they deeply regretted their flaw. An intern who had been with the department for barely a week carelessly generated the letter. The intern mistakenly interpreted the out-of-state certificate as a foreign certificate obtained from a university outside of the United States and was, therefore, not accredited. Kim obtained her master's degree from one of the state universities, and all state universities were accredited institutions of higher learning. Kim was declared as qualified for the position, and her score was ninety-eight points for education and experience combined, plus an additional two promotional points. Kim was hysterical, and she could hardly hold herself up. She walked up and down with the feeling of bitterness over the injustices done to her. It hurt her feelings so badly that she decided to let Devon know. Kim quickly picked up the phone and called him to share the news with him.

After she was put through to Devon, she started saying aloud, "I knew it. I knew it. No one has the right to take this away from me."

"Calm down. Calm down. What's that you are talking about?"

Devon was worried. His first reaction was that Kim might have learned about his affair with another mistress in the D.C. area. He soon suspected that Big Daddy could be the only one to leak that one out. That was the wildest thought he'd had for a long time. Big Daddy didn't reveal friends' secrets, but he shared a friend's fiancée just the way he managed the secret.

"My scores. My scores. Can't you see? Who else can beat me in this?"

Devon's heart finally settled down. "I'm glad you made it. What's the score again?"

"It's hundred points solid. A perfect score of 100 percent ever registered by human resources. Oh my goodness. Oh Lord. Gracious Jesus. I love you, Jesus." She was overjoyed.

Devon heard her crying. "That deserves a celebration, honey, but, unfortunately, I'm not there to throw you one."

He was wrong at this point. What he didn't know was that "the River Mississippi never dries." Immediately after she hung up without saying "I love you" to Devon, Kim drove away to meet Big Daddy at their secret hangout rendezvous to celebrate what Devon couldn't offer her at that time of need.

"I never expected you could come here tonight," said Big Daddy.

"I have followed my Big Daddy. I go wherever you are." Before Big Daddy could respond, she continued, "I am here to celebrate the night with you."

"What occasion is that for?" asked Big Daddy.

She promptly began to relate how the whole human resources, including its commissioner, apologized to her for erroneously disqualifying her for the position of program manager in their first letter. She talked about the perfect hundred-point score for the position and how she looked forward to getting the job. Big Daddy was always the ladies' man. He congratulated her and gave her a breathtaking, long hug, the kind Kim was longing for. She never had that kind of warm hug from Devon, and that very one made her even more intimate with Big Daddy. The difference, however, was that Big Daddy had a massive chest. Every hug Kim got from him gave her a coveted body insulation, compared to Devon with a much lighter body frame. Kim never mentioned her fiancé whenever she was with Big Daddy. She had to realize where her relationship with Big Daddy was heading, but she never cared. She felt secure whenever she was with Big Daddy.

Kim received an invitation letter to attend an interview for the position two weeks from the date of the letter. She let Devon know she was scheduled for an interview and wanted him to influence the decision of the three members on the selection panel so she could be favorably considered for the position.

She called Devon early that morning. "Honey, please call the assistant commissioner about this lifetime opportunity. I know you can do it. Please, honey, do it for me. I have waited for this opportunity all my life," she pleaded.

"Okay, sweetie. I will try. That's not a promise, but first give me the number and name of the person."

Kim was in a hurry and so confused that she gave him Big Daddy's secret cell phone number. Devon called the number the following morning to help push her case. The phone rang twice. Big Daddy never bothered to check the caller. After all, no person other than Kim had that number.

"Hello, dear. What's up?"

Then he heard Devon's voice. "Whom am I speaking with, please? I would like to speak with the assistant commissioner."

Devon was not aware Big Daddy had picked up the call.

Big Daddy pretended as though he was someone else. "Wrong number, sir." He hastily hung up the phone.

Devon called that number again twice, but never again did Big Daddy answer his call. He started sweating. That same day, Big Daddy called the service provider to cancel that contract, remove his name from the record, and assign him another brand-new phone with a different account number. Devon never suspected anything. He called Kim at her workplace to verify if the number she gave him was the correct one.

"Hi, sweetie. I tried the number you gave me yesterday, but the receiver said it was a wrong number."

"Could you please read the number for me, honey?"

He read the number aloud.

Those numbers made her think, "Oh God, not again."

She almost dropped the phone, but she quickly composed herself and said instantaneously, "I'm sorry. That wasn't the right number."

She stopped and waited to hear if he had actually talked to Big Daddy. Fortunately, there was nothing suspicious. She felt a little easier and gave him the correct number to the assistant commissioner's office.

Devon called the assistant commissioner's office. The secretary answered the call.

"I am Congressman Devon. I would like to speak with the assistant commissioner, please."

"Sorry, sir. The assistant commissioner is out of the office."

"Any idea when he will be back?"

"No, sir, but he's on a trip lasting at least a week." The secretary was very polite.

Devon appreciated her professionalism. "Thank you, ma'am. I will call again when he's back. I appreciate your help."

"You are most welcome, sir."

They hung up. Devon never had the chance to speak with the assistant commissioner again. The long congressional session kept him very busy, and that contributed to a straining of a relationship with Kim, who then focused on his areas of weakness to launch her premeditated attacks on him.

Kim attended the interview, but was not selected for the position. Surprisingly, Natalie was offered the position. Kim went nuts. She met with her friends Martha, Annette, Keri'a, and Delores. Then she started blasting the administration and Natalie as well.

"This is a shame in the first place for this department not to consider me for the position. For them to offer the position to that ex-nun is even despicable and outrageous. This is DCS. Our philosophy is to protect children and not to destroy them. Where is the justice if someone who once destroyed her own child is made to care for the children of others?"

Kim slammed Natalie at length and told her friends everything about Natalie's past and her hatred for Natalie. Kim even said that Natalie was not fit to live in the society, allegedly for fear that she might harm the children in the neighborhood.

"That is too much information. How did you come to learn about her so well?" Martha asked.

"To succeed, you must know your enemy well," Kim replied.

"Is she currently married?" Annette asked.

"Natalie is a dead turbine. She couldn't be turned on once again." The girls burst into laughter.

"She needs some greasy lubricant and tune-ups. Ha!" Martha added.

They laughed again. Kim had found the support group who shared her defiant lifestyle. Her four friends, except Delores, had applied for that position.

"Why was she picked?" Keri'a asked the group.

"The assistant commissioner was once her cousin's boyfriend." Kim shook her right hand with every word.

"I learned she once worked in a daycare center as a manager. Was that right?" Annette asked.

"That much I don't know, but she has been around for longer than any one of us, enough to be considered by the administration as an insider or a clique if you will," Kim said.

"It doesn't make sense to me. Please correct me if I'm wrong, but the right place for Natalie should have been the Supermax prison," said Martha.

"She wasn't found guilty. She never resisted what the priest did to her, even the time he ordered her into his bed. All she had to do was hold a rosary in both hands and say, 'Lord, please forgive him. He doesn't know what he is doing.' The prayers ended with her getting pregnant." Kim halted for a few seconds. "Halloo! Is it Saudi Arabia where women have no rights? Or in Cambodia where women know sex better than cooking? That was exactly what the church did to those poor nuns who were trapped behind those huge walls called Maria Immaculate." Kim paused.

The ladies were more attentive than ever before.

"We reserve manpower for national defense in this great nation of ours, but the church reserves woman power for what they called the holy sex. They considered sex between nuns and priests as doctrinaire and therefore blessed. Holy molly!" Kim finally stopped after her lengthy comments.

"Woo!" exclaimed Keri'a, an African immigrant working in the department. She spoke with a heavy Ma'di accent. "I like the African priests. They lead their normal lives as though legalized by the Pope to raise families of their own behind the scene. The society doesn't even care anymore."

Delores, a Hispanic lady who sat next to Keri'a, instantly joined in the conversation, "Ah-ah, nada or no, Iglesias Catoleco does not do that in my—" She paused for while. "Pais! Uh-uh, country, but a priest can give a kiss on the cheek here to a nun during the day and some blessings down there in the night.'" Despite the language barrier, Delores managed to explain to her friends about the eccentrics of the secretive sex in the church.

"Thank you, mistress," said Martha. "That explains the universal phenomena about the mistreatment of female. I guarantee you ladies that women are not safe wherever they happen to be, not even in the Vatican City. It is up to us to stand up for our rights and the rights of those poor children we tend to protect. Am I being right?"

With one voice, the ladies said, "Right! Go, girls. DCS! DCS! Woo! Woo!"

"You know what, girls? Perhaps Natalie is right. Her decision to join this department was a sort of solidarity to our efforts in protecting the children and, furthermore, repentance and reconciliation with her past," Martha concluded.

"Whatever. I went through that once when I got pregnant to my own cousin brother and concealed it. Why can't she?" Annette declared.

"Hello, ladies! We aren't here to reveal secrets or confess. Do y'all understand what I'm saying?" said Kim as the group started getting out of hand.

The commotion died down.

"I'm married to my sister's former boyfriend. And what's your big story, Kim?" Martha said provocatively to get Kim to talk about how she ended up with her friend's boyfriend.

"Ugh, that is disgusting. How would you possibly do something like that?" Keri'a said.

"Aw yeah. Disgusting or not, I did it, and I survived the consequences. Now he belongs to me." Martha pointed the thumbs toward her.

"I have no comments to that kind of mess. It's too personal." Kim declined from telling her part of the story.

Perhaps that was a wise decision. She couldn't afford to let everyone talk about her afterwards. The ladies hung together for quite some time. One by one, they left for the night.

Kim didn't schedule a date with Big Daddy that evening. She went straight to her apartment. To her surprise, Devon was home. He had arrived unannounced. Kim could call herself so lucky that Big Daddy never called that night. Neither did he show up as he used to do in the past. Kim was upset because Devon didn't push her case through. He, however, explained to her how difficult it was to get in touch with the assistant commissioner. Besides, Devon was a member of the Congressional Ethics Committee. For him to act unethically would raise many questions, let alone jeopardize his own seat in the next election. They discussed a range of issues, and Devon finally managed to convince her before they went to bed for the rest of the night.

Progress had not been made in the Child Protection Unit since Kim took over as its supervisor. Her five staff members were stressed. Some had already considered moving out of the unit. Amy, fortunately, got married to her college sweetheart. She would move out of the state to live with her husband at the military base in Las Cruces, New Mexico. She tendered her resignation, but promised to keep her workmates in heart even if she wouldn't meet with them anytime soon. Kim was very sad. She felt like her unit would fall apart because Amy was the only person among the group who had at least maintained some sort of low-key friendship with her. Kim organized a farewell party for Amy at her apartment, but, unfortunately, all the other unit staff didn't show up. Kim ended up with Amy, two of her girlfriends, and Vicky, who joined the group late that night. They spent time together until midnight when Amy and Vicky decided to leave. They left behind Kim and her two friends, who were still discussing men and their big plans.

Amy's departure from Child Protection Unit created a staff shortage that was not easy to fill. Her job assignments were, however, distributed between Tina and Reggie because Steve and Vicky were already overloaded. The director tried to transfer one employee from another unit to temporarily fill the position that Amy vacated, but she declined because she had already known Kim as an arrogant supervisor. The worker fervently resisted her transfer under Kim's supervision. She openly warned that she would rather quit her job than join the Child Protection Unit. Steve, Reggie, and Tina vowed never to abandon their unit, and they repeatedly told Kim never to think that her mistreatment and arrogance would force them to change their minds. Reggie even proposed a campaign throughout the department to have Kim removed from the unit, but Steve and Tina advised her that it was illegal and insubordination to wage such a campaign against one's own supervisor. They instead planned a constructive engagement where they would make their concerns known to Kim in every single unit meeting. They consistently started doing that, and Kim gradually began to close the gap between them. She opened up and started listening to them. She occasionally asked for their suggestions and feedback. The plan worked. Changes gradually started taking place. The big surprise came when Kim, for the first time, publicly apologized to them for all what had happened in the unit. She promised to cooperate and work together with them in order to bring about change that her unit most needed. The unit members accepted Kim's apology. After all the wild roller coaster rides with her staff, Kim finally breathed the fresh air of freedom and love of the employees. She opened up her heart to them in a way never seen before.

"Who would ever believe that Kim could change to an extent of embracing ideas from us?" Reggie commented immediately after their meeting.

"Because we never gave up on her, and that impacted her perception," said Tina.

"Precisely right. Fleeing is not a solution to our problems. The persuasive approach we adopted seemed to have worked well, and I'm grateful to get our unit getting back. That was a team effort, so congratulations to each one of you," Steve lamented in a very professional way.

"I'm sorry if I had been part of the problem, but I'm still part of the team. I would do whatever it takes to make sure the future journey would always be made together," Vicky confessed to the group.

"Thank you, Vicky, for the nice comments. We haven't rejected you as part of us. Besides, we were one happy family before Kim joined this unit." Tina moved close to Vicky and hugged her.

Reggie and Steve followed shortly after. The four had now joined in forces as a team and would once again get their unit going in the right direction.

Chapter Seven

The Reconciliation Phases

Not only had Kim's unprecedented turnaround surprised her staff, she had her name on everyone's lips in the entire department. The constructive engagement approach that the staff of her unit had taken opened the opportunity for new life at the workplace and beyond. Kim went to Natalie and apologized for what she said about her some months ago. "I am so sorry for the comments I made about you last time. Please forgive me for my inappropriate statement. You deserve better."

Natalie felt sorry for her and quickly accepted the apology. "We are human beings. We do make mistakes that we at times do not intend to. I have forgiven you that same day, and that is why I am able to move on with my daily life.

The sequence of events had taken a wide spectrum. Kim thought of reconciling with Katie. Katie had moved out of her apartment and lived for some time with a crack head cousin who happily welcomed Katie in her house on the condition of not interfering with her addiction. Katie agreed because she knew her presence could make a difference in her cousin's life. She worked relentlessly to help the cousin change her addiction habits. The young cousin gradually started responding to her advice and began showing some positive signs of recovery. After nearly a year of grueling effort, the cousin finally got out of her drug addiction. The cousin remained close to Katie and regarded her as her hero. She got a new job at the grocery store after nearly two years after she was laid off from her last job when her company shut down. She was the only child for her father. When her father died, she became frustrated and started doing drugs. Luckily enough, she inherited her father's properties, the house, cars, and all the monies in his bank accounts.

The channel of communication between Kim and members of her unit had improved tremendously. As a result, Kim no longer decided on plans without prior consultation with her staff members, especially Steve, who had the greatest influence upon other staff members. Kim was pressing for a training program for her unit, and she had asked her staff to come up with some plans for the training. They planned that Kim and Steve should attend effective supervision practices for lower and middle management. The other three needed the child protection management training. According to the plan, both training should be conducted once a week for over a period of three months. The proposal was presented to the director and subsequently approved. That was the first project Kim had initiated and successfully worked on jointly with her staff. It was a big leap forward for Kim. That training, together with practical supervision, helped Kim a lot in making fair judgments and application of appropriate behavioral approach at the workplace. Kim became an outspoken woman on ethics reform in the whole department, a lesson she herself learned from the field.

With Judy and a few other long-serving employees gone into retirement, Kim had finally positioned herself for yet another promotional showdown. Her complete turnaround served her well, and she was recommended for another promotion in a different unit. She, however, convinced the director and had the position transferred to the Child Protection Unit and with her as the head. Her former position fell vacant for quite some time. Steve later filled it. Reggie also got a promotion as case manager three in the same unit. Tina and Vicky remained on the register for a case manager three position. They, however, had opportunities to move forward in one of the units under DCS, if not within their own unit where they had worked for the last five years or so.

Vicky was delighted when she received an e-mail from Amy stating she was pregnant and they were expecting their first baby in five months. Vicky happily shared that news during their monthly unit meeting. She also gave them Amy's new e-mail address and encouraged them to chat with her online should they have some free time at home.

"Oh, she finally wrote again. It had been like four months without hearing from her," Vicky said with relief.

"I'm excited to hear from her, too," Reggie responded.

"What's she doing? Has she gotten a job or not?" asked Tina.

"Probably not yet. Her pregnancy would have prevented her from searching for one," said Vicky.

"That's understandable. She made the right decision, especially with her first pregnancy," Kim stated. "We should send her a card."

"That's a good idea," said Steve.

"I'll get the card and have everybody sign it so it could be mailed out promptly," said Kim.

Vicky volunteered to send it on behalf of the group. Kim brought the card the next morning. Everyone signed it. Vicky sent it during her lunch break. She told the group that the mail had gone. She looked forward to hearing from Amy once she received it. The members of the Child Protection Unit hung together for lunch like never before. Kim sometimes joined them at her favorite restaurant, which wasn't far from the office building. They organized a feeding frenzy at different occasions and birthday cakes to celebrate the birthday of every staff member of the unit. Harmony had surely taken roots in the unit that disintegration once threatened.

The election year was around the corner. Devon asked Kim and Big Daddy to help with the organization of the election campaigns and, of course, the fund-raising parties as well. He called Kim to let her know that he would be in the town for some preliminary arrangements in about two weeks. Devon also contacted Big Daddy about fund-raising and some personal contributions. Kim and Big Daddy were no longer intimate as they used to be. Her sacrifice to transform herself into a better person made her change her attitude toward her relationship with Big Daddy. She turned down several dates with him, and she told him they should better stop seeing each other for the sake of Big Daddy's marriage and her relationship with Devon. Big Daddy welcomed her decision and honored it wholeheartedly. They, however, agreed to maintain their family friendship. Kim requested two months of annual leave to focus on Devon's election campaign. She planned to round up several counties together with Devon and then make some additional tours by herself when Devon was scheduled for a series of city hall meetings.

Chapter Eight

The Election Season

The general elections had finally kicked off. Kim was released to take part in the campaign for Devon, who had already arrived in his constituency two days ahead of time. She and Devon scheduled several meetings together. Big Daddy also had organizing several fund-raising parties in some big cities. He had a strong base with the business communities in several counties and the state capital.

Devon's campaign manager was himself once a congressman for two terms when he called it quits to take care of his business. Devon had laid a good ground organization, abundant campaign funds, and grassroots mobilization teams. The passage of Devon's unemployment benefits bill had touched so many hearts in his home state that the high unemployment rate had devastated. The election season seemed to have arrived just in time. The electorates would show how much the state and its entire population appreciated his efforts and support to the state.

Steve, Reggie, Tina, and Vicky all volunteered in voter registration to boost Devon's chances of winning. Kim was overwhelmed to see them donating their after-work times and weekends as well.

"Man! Mr. Devon is gonna win this election by a landslide of votes. He has good organization and manpower all around," said Steve.

"I'm sure he is. People seem to like him, especially after the passage of the unemployment benefits bill," said Vicky.

"We wish him the best. Perhaps his success would answer many of the state's problems." Steve continued to read some of the pressing problems facing the state like unemployment, high rates of school dropouts, teachers' salaries, obesity, health insurance for unemployed families, and many others.

"Don't leave out the state budget cuts, please," Tina added.

"Yes, that's one area I should have started with. Thanks for reminding me," said Steve.

They moved from one door to another around the neighborhoods. Reggie and Tina were asked to remain behind in the campaign office to help with phone calls to voters. That also left Steve and Vicky to work together while registering in the neighborhoods.

Working in pairs was always a good thing because the two got to know each other better. That was what happened between Vicky and Steve. Steve learned that Vicky was a beautiful young lady who had no hurry for everything. They would knock at the voter's door. The occupant would take fifteen to twenty minutes to respond, but Vicky would always say, "Let's be patient and wait. It's the election year, and voters are aware that we need their votes. They would do anything to discourage us to leave."

They would stand by the door and wait and wait. At times, their patience would pay off.

One of the occupants would show up and say, "I'm sorry for keeping you waiting for so long. I was in the bathroom, and there was no one to open the door. How can I help you?"

Then the two would introduce themselves and state the reason why they were there. With the voter's permission, Steve and Vicky would put the name down as a potential supporter and proceed to the next door. Vicky also saw Steve as someone forgiving, friendly, and accommodative. She had, in fact, admired his good personality all the years they had worked together in Child Protection Unit, even at the downturn of events following Kim's arrival. Day in and day out, Steve and Vicky roamed the neighborhoods together.

One evening, Vicky asked Steve to join her for dinner at her apartment, and he accepted. It was a Saturday evening after they had registered voters for the whole day. Vicky and Steve called it a day, and Vicky took Steve to her apartment. "Welcome to my apartment Steve." She said as they got into the living room.

"Thank you for inviting me, you have a nice apartment." Steve said as he took seat in a couch.

"I know it would sound rather stupid, but I have to ask. Would you like to take a shower after the long day walk canvassing the neighborhoods?" Steve was hesitant, but finally accepted after making some joking remarks.

"Let me make sure your boyfriend isn't somewhere around."

"You are the only man who has entered my apartment so far. Just feel free to inspect the house even before you take off your shoes."

"I believe you. I was just joking."

He left the living room and went into the bathroom. Vicky had broken up with her boyfriend because of unnecessary demands, including sex on their first date. She became afraid of him, so she decided to leave her previous apartment without even letting the boyfriend know her whereabouts. Since then, the two never saw each other again. Steve took fifteen minutes in the bathroom. Vicky was busy in the kitchen, warming some food for dinner. Then, one by one, she arranged them on the table. The dinner was ready when Steve came out of the shower. Barefoot, he walked slowly toward the living room to join Vicky, who kept smiling as he approached.

"Thank you very much. Now I feel fresh," said Steve.

"That's better. I knew you were exhausted."

"It's your turn now."

"Are you sure we don't have to have dinner first?"

"No, I'm in no hurry. Go ahead and take a shower. I will wait for you."

"Just take some food, please."

"No, we will better have it together."

She left. Within five minutes, she was done and called for Steve to hand her another towel from her dresser. Steve got the towel from one of the drawers and took it to the bathroom where Vicky was waiting behind the transparent shower curtain. Steve gave her the towel, and she received it from over the curtain. She came out of the bathroom in her robe and immediately asked Steve to move to the dining room table.

They ate and talked a great deal. She told him everything about herself, including her latest boyfriend. Steve also told her that he wasn't seeing anyone at the time. He had planned to stay that way after his girlfriend disappointed him and ran away with another man.

"What were you doing when she decided to run away with another man?" Vicky asked.

"I'm the guy who always like to have things done right."

"And you ended up paying the ultimate price, didn't you?"

"I for sure did."

"What's your next move?"

"No idea at all at this time. Maybe I should lay low and wait for the right moment to come."

"That's interesting." She smiled.

"I guess so." He smiled back.

Vicky smiled, too. "What's your plan for tonight?"

"Nothing special. Crawl into my miserable bed and sleep."

"How about going to the movie theatre? Do you like movies?"

"I do, but not tonight."

"If not tonight, then when?"

"You choose one for me."

Vicky smiled. "I love that."

"What's that you loved?"

"What you have just said." She laughed aloud this time.

Steve joined in the laughter.

"Let's move back to the living room." She grabbed his hand and led him into the living room.

Both settled close to one another.

"What's the best thing a gentleman could do for a lady?" She still held his hand in both hands.

Steve thought for a while. "To be at her service for whatever she asks."

"Good answer." She moved closer and kissed him.

"What's that for?"

"For you being a gentleman." She kissed him again.

They kissed again and again. Vicky seemed to have finally found a place in his heart, and she was also joyful because he didn't disappoint her in her quest for a loving heart. She finally got the man of her dreams.

For the first time, she said to him, "I love you, Steve." She remained glued in his arms.

"I love you, too." Steve drew her even tighter and kissed her again.

"Could you please accompany me to the movie theatre tonight?" Vicky asked.

"At your request, yes I will." He finally gave in, and Vicky hurriedly went to the bedroom and came back well dressed, then together they left for the movie theatre. They went back to Vicky's apartment after the movie and remained together until the late night when Steve decided to leave.

"Could you please stay just a little longer?" she begged him.

"I can't." He responded with sort of sadness.

"Aha! Now you are forgetting the rule you spelled out some hours ago," she joked.

"I'd love to, but you know we have to do some volunteer work tomorrow morning."

"I also need a volunteer around."

He felt sorry. Steve was about to give in and stay longer.

Vicky said, "Promise me that you wouldn't abandon me, please."

"You have my word for that. I promise."

She gave him a good-bye kiss and then let him drive home in her car.

Chapter Nine

The Post-Election Era

Steve and Vicky continued to round up the neighborhood together and registered voters for over a month. Their relationship got stronger and stronger as they spent most of their after-work and weekend hours together. Steve had cautioned not to make it too open for fear of office regulations. Vicky planned to transfer to another unit so they could have the freedom to make their affair more open.

The answer came when Devon won the congressional seat for his district. He was going back to Washington for a second term. He was very impressed with the volunteers' work that made his campaign successful. Kim had suggested he find a position for Steve in his office, and he agreed. Three months later, Steve was invited to Washington to take a new assignment of public relations officer in Devon's Washington office.

He requested a one-week annual leave from the office for his trip, and Kim gladly approved it. He returned from Washington and requested for a release letter. That was also granted. A farewell party was organized in his honor on Friday, where Kim and the director expressed their gratitude and appreciation for his extraordinary and distinguished service in general and the Child Protection Unit in particular. He was awarded with the department's certificate of excellence signed by the commissioner.

That also marked Steve's career service with the Child Protection Unit, where he had worked for about ten years. It was a sad moment for him to leave his co-workers and Vicky. He, however, overcame his anxiety and looked forward to assisting the people wherever he happened to be. He stayed with Vicky after his release from the DCS until the date of his departure to Washington. His departure left a vacancy in the Child Protection Unit that had yet to deal with the loss of another member. With Steve also gone, the staff of the unit would literally shrink to a bare skeleton. Vicky got pregnant and wanted to move to Washington to join Steve. Steve welcomed her pregnancy, but she couldn't move until Steve got an apartment of his own. So Vicky had to stay behind and continue to work for some time.

Devon and Kim finally wed in Washington six months after he won the election in a landslide victory. He attributed his success to Kim, her workmates, and Big Daddy, who remained the powerhouse behind his financial support. He also thanked the campaign manager and all the staff who took part or supported him during the campaign.

Kim invited all her unit members, the director, her close friends, and those who took part in her husband's election campaign. She even extended an invitation to Katie, who turned it down. Katie was still bitter toward Kim for not only destroying her relationship with the congressman, but going as far as marrying him. She promised never to see Kim again for the rest of her life. That, however, changed after Devon apologized to her and asked for forgiveness. She reluctantly did forgive him. She also forgave Kim and asked her to forget the past and open up a new chapter in her life. They eventually got back as friends once again. Since then, both Kim and Katie maintained an open channel of communication and, at times, visited one another. Katie got engaged to Kyle, a former NBA star who coached an NBA team. They lived together in a gated affluent community of Sunrise City, and both looked forward to their forthcoming wedding scheduled for midsummer.

Vicky sent an e-mail to Amy to inform her she was carrying Steve's baby and the wedding of Kim to Devon. She told Amy many stories, including some new developments in the department. The following Saturday morning, Amy called Vicky for a lengthy discussion.

"Hi. It's nice to hear your voice again. How are you and the baby doing?" asked Vicky.

"We are doing just fine. How about yourself and the baby?" asked Amy.

"Giving me kinda hard time, but I guess we're doing just fine."

"You'll get used to it. I had a hard time adjusting in my fifth month of pregnancy."

"Thank God that I'm getting all the help I need from Steve's sister. She even asked me to move in with them, as Steve suggested."

"That sounds great. What are you waiting for?"

"My apartment contract ends in three months. I'll consider it after the contract is over. That way, I'll have my deposit back."

"How's Steve?"

"I guess he's doing fine. I talked to him this morning." Her voice was shaky, and she felt like crying.

"Are you crying?" Amy realized that Vicky was not comfortable.

"Never mind. I'll be fine. I just miss him. That's probably why I became emotional." Vicky cleared her throat and regained her voice.

"My husband will be deployed to Iraq for twelve months next month. We decided I should stay with my parents while he's away. My parents and my in-laws agreed on that arrangement, and I will probably come down there with him before he leaves. I'm excited because we will be together once again."

Vicky was very delighted, too. "That's the good news I have been waiting for so long. We will be here waiting for you."

Before she could finish her sentence, someone was on the line. She put Amy on hold. It was Steve again. "Hello, Vicky speaking." She answered. "Hi honey, this is me again—." Before he could continue any further, Vicky said. "Darling please hang up, I'm on line with Amy. I will call you back after I am through with her." She hung up. Then she got back to Amy.

"That was Steve. I told him to hang up and I'd get back to him when we are done."

"You shouldn't have done that. You better get back with him right out, and I will call in the evening."

Vicky wouldn't let her go, so they continued to chat for another thirty minutes.

Devon assigned Steve an urgent mission to follow up on certain issues in his constituency for one week. Steve had wanted to tell Vicky that he was on his way home and he would be with her in three hours. Vicky tried to call, but Steve couldn't answer because he was already on board the plane. Vicky was worried. She thought Steve was disappointed when she couldn't call him back. She sat in the middle of her bed with her cell phone tightly clenched in the right hand for about an hour when the doorbell rang. She rose slowly and dragged herself to the door.

"Vicky!" Wynona, Steve's sister, called.

Vicky opened the door and welcomed her in. She was relieved for Wynona's arrival. As usual, Wynona went to the kitchen area and started cleaning from there to the bathroom and then the living area. She prepared some soup for Vicky before she settled down to chat.

"How are you feeling today?" asked Wynona.

"Not any better, but it's part of me for now until the time comes." Vicky tried to sit upright, but couldn't.

"Positive attitude? Ha!"

Vicky smiled and then said in an appreciative tone, "You mean everything to me." She held Wynona's right hand tightly, kissed it, and smiled.

"That's what a sister-in-law is for. I feel it's my responsibility to help you. You know my brother is not around to give you the help and support you need."

"Thanks for being so nice to me. I know Steve could give me a hand, but I never miss the help I need. You are always here for me."

"You will do the same for me when I'm in your situation."

Wynona talked about her family background. Their grandfather was a World War II veteran. Their father was a retired air force pilot during the Gulf War. Their mother was a middle school headmistress. As they were talking, the doorbell rang.

Wynona asked, "Are you expecting a guest?"

"No."

They were about to ignore the bell when it rang repeatedly. Wynona opened the door. She screamed at the top of her voice when she saw Steve at the door. She hugged him and led him into the living room. Vicky sprang up and hugged Steve. She kissed him countless times. Then they settled into the couch for more kisses.

"Why didn't you answer my phone?" she asked.

"I was on the plane. I tried to tell you of my journey, but you cut me short."

"I'm so sorry. I didn't know you were about to tell me of your trip."

"No, that's fine. I'm glad that I'm here now."

"I was with Amy on phone, and I put him on hold when you called. I'm sorry, I wish I gave you the chance to tell me of your trip." She apologized for not getting back with him sooner.

Wynona left Steve and Vicky talking in the living room. She went to the kitchen to prepare some food for Steve. That was what she always did whenever her elder brother came home to visit them. She never let Steve leave the house without having food. She came back into the living room and joined Steve and Vicky. She took a seat opposite where the two were sitting.

"Why didn't you call to let me pick you up from the airport?" asked Wynona.

"I'm sorry about that, but I got a ride from a friend who happened to be at the airport. Thank you though."

"It was my fault. He tried to tell me, but I never gave him the chance to do so. I'm so sorry." She looked at Steve and smiled.

"You don't need to say that, honey. Things worked out perfectly well. I got a ride. I wouldn't have asked you to pick me up because of your condition."

"Ah! You are so sweet." Vicky kissed him repeatedly before she leaned her back against the sofa.

"Mom and I talked about you yesterday," said Wynona.

"Oh really! What was it all about?" Steve said.

"It was all about moving Vicky in with us. Mom wanted to talk with you about it once again."

"I appreciate that. We'll talk about it because I'm here. How is Mom doing?"

"She's doing great. Dad, too." Wynona left for the kitchen to prepare lunch.

She got it ready and came back to tell Steve and Vicky to get some. The three sat at the table and continued their discussions as they ate.

"What unannounced business are you here for, brother?" asked Wynona.

"I have my fiancée, my sister, and the parents here that I can't afford to miss for so long," he joked.

The comments thrilled both Vicky and Wynona.

"I have news for you." Vicky paused and then turned slightly toward Steve.

"I'm listening."

"Amy is coming back to town next month."

Steve thought Amy was having some problems with her marriage. "Why so soon? Is the marriage over?"

"Of course not. She's coming to stay with the parents. Her husband is being deployed for one year in Iraq."

Vicky later said that Amy would come with her husband before he left for Iraq. She wished Steve would be around to meet them when they came. Steve said he would have no problem coming down over the weekend if they would be around during one of the weekends. She also said that Kim visited two weeks ago and brought her a basket of fruit. She told him about her upcoming doctor's appointment as well.

"I will go with you if I'm still around," said Steve.

"I can go with her, like the last time," said Wynona.

"I appreciate that, baby sister. Let me go this time."

"We can all go together. How's that?" said Wynona.

"Sure we can. We will pick you up on our way to the hospital," said Steve.

"I'll be ready waiting for you that day," she said.

The doorbell rang. Wynona went to check who was there. Kim was carrying a large basket of fruit for Vicky. She and Wynona exchanged greetings at the door. Wynona let her in. She was surprised to see Steve sitting on the chair next to Vicky. She walked straight to them, placed the basket on the table, and hugged Vicky and Steve before she could take a seat next to Vicky.

"What a surprise! How did you come without letting us know?"

"My trip was decided at the last minute. Devon never let me know until this morning."

"He talked about sending you down here, but never talked on some specifics on the nature of the mission. Anyway, we're pleased to see you around for some days," said Kim.

"That's right. I will be around for a week, and I will have plenty of time to go out together for dinner," said Steve.

Kim nodded her head. "We sure will. It has been so long. We haven't had dinner together."

"What would you like to drink, ma'am?" asked Wynona.

"No thanks. I had some juice on my way here."

Vicky asked the group to go to the living room as Wynona cleared the dining table. Steve and Vicky sat on the couch. Kim took a seat on the sofa facing them.

"Tell me. How's Washington?" asked Kim.

"Very crazy. Everybody is very busy out there," replied Steve.

"That's expected, especially with the House in session," said Kim.

"I know, but we are keeping up with it," he said.

"And we become the victims back here." Vicky simply wanted to express her thought on how she and Kim felt when Devon and Steve were away in Washington.

"I understand your concerns. It's kinda hard on our side as well, but, at times, we have to sacrifice in order to achieve some of our goals," said Steve.

"Absolutely right. That's exactly what Dee tells me every time I complain of loneliness," said Kim.

Wynona joined the group after cleaning the dining area. She took a seat next to Kim. "Can you tell me your name once again please? I'm Wynona." She extended her hand for a handshake.

"I'm Kim Killinga. They call me Ms. KK." Kim still held Wynona's hand.

"Thank you, Ms. KK. What a nice name?"

Kim let her hand go.

"That's my baby sister."

Wynona smiled at his remarks.

"You preempted what I was about to ask. You have such a beautiful sister." Kim hugged Wynona, who was sitting next to her.

They hung together and discussed on a range of topics. At one point, Steve talked about Devon's recent appointment as chairman of the Ethics Committee and his assignment to meet with the local chairman to collect some data on violation and misuse of powers by public officials in the state.

"That is a very sensitive issue. You don't have to share it with anybody, not even with me, his wife," Kim advised.

Steve listened carefully and said to himself, "Okay, she has a point there. If the congressman didn't tell her about my mission, perhaps he trusted me more in handling this case."

He got back to Kim. "If you say so, that is fine with me. After all, we haven't met with the local chairman yet."

He had come to know how helpful Kim was and had even come to know Devon even better through her. It was already evening. Steve asked Wynona to get them some drinks at a nearby grocery store. Steve, Kim, and Vicky continued with their discussions unabated. Kim urged Steve to make good of his position and use it as leverage for his future career. She wanted Steve to become a politician and fulfill his future dreams.

"Listen to me, Steve. Politicians are not born. They are created by the very people they rule, and you are not any different from them."

Steve listened carefully. For him, it was like an out-of-reach territory that had never crossed his mind before. He, however, didn't object to what she said. Vicky excused herself and went to the bathroom. Wynona came back with some drinks and groceries.

"Do you need any help?"

"No," she said.

She quickly went back after placing the bags on the kitchen counter. She came back and locked the door behind her.

"That was quick," said Kim.

"Yeah, I used the express self-service register for checkout. Not many customers there today." She smiled. "Budgets are tight."

Steve and Kim laughed at her remark.

"I do that all the time, especially when I have fewer items," said Kim.

Steve excused himself and went to the kitchen. He came back with two bottles of beer. He handed one to Kim. "Do you need a glass, Madame KK?"

Wynona quietly rose from her seat and went toward the kitchen.

"Yes, I do, Steve," replied Kim.

Before he could get her one, Wynona came with two glasses and placed them on the table. "Just in case you may also need one, brother." She said.

Vicky came back and sat close to Steve.

"Thank you, baby sister." Steve rose and emptied Kim's bottle in her cup. He asked her to serve herself.

"Thanks, Steve. You're such a nice gentleman," she said.

"See! That's how I look at you all the time whenever you serve me." Said Vicky.

Steve smiled. "Being nice to someone is priceless. Besides, you deserve that treatment."

Kim and Vicky both laughed.

"You also do know that. Ha!" commented Kim.

"I guess so," said Steve.

"Yes, you do." Vicky moved closer to him.

Kim sipped her beer slowly. She was a careful woman who didn't make excuses when it came to traffic regulations. She made it clear that driving after consumption of beer was not only a traffic violation, but an endangerment of public safety comparable to suicide. She had also become extra vigilant not to tarnish Devon's reputation by being pulled over for drunk driving.

She drank a glass halfway. "Wynona, can you empty the glass in the sink?"

"You haven't drunk it even halfway yet," Steve said.

"I liked it that much. I have to drive home."

"But one bottle wouldn't make you drunk," said Steve.

"Not for cops, Steve."

"You are right. They arrest drivers even for any empty bottles found in their car," said Steve.

Vicky was curious. "What did you just say? Even empty bottles of shampoo?"

"That's right. Hazardous materials aren't needed in cars anymore," he joked.

"Don't listen to my brother. He's teasing you." Wynona said.

Vicky squeezed Steve against her. "You freaked me out, honey."

"Sorry, I didn't mean to. It was just a joke," he admitted.

All laughed. Kim stayed with the group until late in the night when she finally decided to go home. Steve and Vicky saw Kim off at the parking lot. Then they went back into the house.

Steve stayed busy with his schedule the following week. He met with the local party politicians in five different counties before settling down on the fourth day to put the reports together. His conflicting schedules made it even harder for him to visit his parents. On Wynona's insistence, however, Steve cancelled some of his appointments. One evening after Vicky's appointment, Steve, Vicky, and Wynona drove to the parents' home. They were out at the time, but Wynona welcomed them home.

"Mom and Dad left this morning to visit a family friend. I thought they'd be home by now."

She lived with her parents, but also spent some time assisting Vicky during the day. She brought two glasses of orange juice for Steve and Vicky. Wynona called her mom's cell phone to inform them that Steve and Vicky were at home and waiting for them to come. Her mom said they would not come home anytime soon because they had gone out of town with their family friends. Steve asked Wynona to hand the cell phone over to him. He talked with both of his parents and then hung up.

Steve asked, "Can we go to Kim's house? She's expecting us."

Vicky and Wynona agreed. Then the three left for Kim's house.

Kim was at home expecting Steve and the two ladies. She planned to take them out for dinner that night. She rushed to the door when the doorbell rang. Kim welcomed Steve and the two ladies into the house. The beautiful interior of the house overwhelmed Wynona. She saw the curtains, the elegant chairs, and all what her eyes could come across.

"Wow! You have such a wonderful apartment," Wynona said.

"Do you like it?" Kim asked

"Everyone would like it," Wynona answered.

Kim was flattered. Her effort for years had paid off with those sweet comments from Wynona.

"Could we go to the dinner at one of the finest restaurants in the city?

"I guess we could," responded Steve.

Kim offered to give them a ride in her luxury Lincoln SUV.

"You have a nice truck, too." Wynona said after taking her seat.

"Really! Thank you for the compliment," Kim said.

"Try to work hard, and you will get one like hers, baby sister," Steve said.

"Yes, you also need to have a great man behind you," Vicky added.

Kim pulled out of the apartment complex. She slowly drove past the quiet neighborhood. She turned on a busy freeway and then headed on their way to the urban area where most of the businesses were located. She passed several restaurants before she stopped at one of her favorites, the Millennium.

Very few state employees could afford to dine in that restaurant. In fact, they didn't even know the restaurant ever existed. Every food in that restaurant was prepared to the customer's taste. Its customers neither complained of the services nor the food being served, but there was the prices and the 25 percent additional charges levied on every order as tips. The food was great. Kim entertained her guests with respect and honor to the extent that Steve intervened to shoulder part of the cost, but Kim rejected his offer. She paid for everything that night, including tickets for the movie. They went back to Kim's apartment after the movie and stayed there until the early morning hours.

Steve was left with two days to wrap up his mission. He scheduled several meetings and visits with local county councils before he could leave for Washington. He met with some state representatives and community leaders in separate occasions. He went to his parents' home twice in a row and had a dinner party in his honor at Vicky's apartments in the company of Kim, Tina, Reggie, and her boyfriend. His parents called early in the day to inform him that they wouldn't be available for the farewell party due to other programs. Steve was very grateful to his former co-workers for showing up that night. He and Reggie's boyfriend barbequed. Wynona and Vicky served the guests. Kim volunteered to provide some beer. Reggie introduced her boyfriend as Rock.

Steve immediately picked on her. "And now you are known as Ms. RR. Is that right?"

"I guess so." Reggie responded.

Tina immediately said, "Ms. KK, Ms. RR, and Ms. VV. Great combinations! What a coincidence!" Tina meant Ms. Kim Killinga, Ms. Reggie Rock, and Ms. Vicky Vincent.

Those names interested Wynona. "Wynona Williams. I'd go by Ms. WW or simply Ms. WiWi. How about you, Tina?"

Her boyfriend's name was called Williams. Steve didn't like Williams much because he wore oversized shirts and walked with his pants down. Wynona tried to persuade Williams to dress like a gentlemen, but he told her that he couldn't dress like the oldies.

"I'm cool with what I wear. Take it, or leave it." He told Wynona.

"I would be forced to look for a man whose name starts with the letter T, like Tyson, Tyron, or Tiger. Then I would become Tina Tyson or Tina Tyron and then eventually referred to as Ms. TT. "

"Wow! That sounds wonderful," Vicky said.

The ladies laughed. The group had a good time together that night.

Kim, Tina, Reggie, and her boyfriend all left Vicky's apartment at the same time. Kim promised to meet Steve again the following morning before he left for the airport. She had a parcel to be delivered to Devon. She had already told Devon that Steve was carrying the parcel.

Before she got into her car, she said to Steve, "Please don't leave before I get here. I want you to deliver a parcel in person to Devon, as I discussed with him over the phone last night."

"You have my word for that. I will wait even if it could mean missing my flight."

Kim was delighted with his response. She smiled. "Thank you. You are the ladies' man, Mr. Steve."

Steve patted Kim on the back. "Not really, ma'am. I just try to be a handy man."

After the assurances from Steve, Kim left for the night. Steve and Vicky also retreated to bed right after Wynona left for the guest room.

Kim went to Vicky's apartment early Sunday morning to meet with Steve. She carried a large parcel that had to be taken to Devon. It contained some documents for an estate that she and Devon planned to acquire through Big Daddy. She instructed Steve to put it in his carry-on bag or briefcase to make sure it got safely into Devon's hands. Steve did exactly as she instructed. He put the parcel in his briefcase.

Kim gave him a thumbs-up. "Good job. Now I'm confident it would get to Dee safely."

She got to her feet and hugged Steve and Vicky. Then she left for church. Steve left for the airport at around two o'clock. His flight was scheduled for four. Vicky and Wynona saw him off at the airport. Then they went to Wynona's parents' home for the rest of the evening.

Four months later, Vicky gave birth to a baby boy and named him Steve Vincent Jr. Wynona moved in with Vicky. She also attended college at a nearby state university. Kim found great love in her marriage. She became pregnant after a desperate struggle to have a child. She was expecting a baby in five months, and Devon visited her quite frequently. He also purchased a dream house for Kim. Amy came back to her hometown when her husband was scheduled to leave for Iraq on military duty.

The unexpected miracle did happen when Big Daddy's wife conceived after seven agonizing years. She planned to name the unborn baby Isaac, after the biblical son of Abraham, but Big Daddy objected categorically. He told her the child should take his name and be called Melvin Woodcock Jr.

"That's my baby. Not Abraham's."

"I have no objection for the baby to take your name, honey. After all, you're his father. I just suggested the name to express my gratitude after those seven long years of childlessness."

Big Daddy and his wife renewed their marriage vows, and he remained faithful to her thereafter. Kim became a born-again Christian. She attended church every single Sunday and taught Sunday school at their local church as well. Ever since, Kim remained a close family friend to Steve and Big Daddy's families.